MAX'S CAMPERVAN CASE FILES BOOK 11

CHRISTMAS CORPSE

TYLER RHODES

Copyright © 2024 Tyler Rhodes

Dedicated to Santa. We love you!

Chapter 1

"I'll open the gate." Min beamed at me, a wicked glint in her eye, as she wrapped a massive multi-coloured scarf around her neck then let it hang down over a very thick, oversized red sweater.

"Thanks." I pulled on the handbrake and sighed happily, then shivered as a blast of icy air buffeted the interior of Vee, my 67 VW Campervan, as Min heaved against the door and battled the frosty Arctic wind. The "heater" had been struggling for hours with the low outside temperatures, and with a click and a whirr clearly figured it may as well give up until the door was closed.

"See you in a mo." Min slammed the door shut and the temperature rose a degree or two so I put my hands in front of the vent and rubbed them together, keen to get settled at the campsite and have the small portable electric heater up and running.

My beautiful ex-wife traipsed across the frozen grass, leaving footprints in her wake. Her heavy boots and thermal socks, combined with the insanely chunky sweater and scarf, made her look like the latest Doctor Who, the red bobble hat and rosy nose completing the festive look. I still couldn't believe it was Christmas Day tomorrow and we were spending it together. It was going to be perfect. Me, Min, and Anxious the adorable Jack Russell Terrier parked up at a remote campsite for a few days over the holiday period with nothing to do but try to stay warm and enjoy each other's company.

Min was struggling with the gate, seemingly unable to get it open, so I took a deep breath then killed the engine and jumped out, steeling myself for the bitter cold that had been a constant for several weeks now. We'd hit as low as minus sixteen Celsius, almost a record for the UK, but today we were up to a balmy minus three and supposedly it was meant to hit plus figures by tomorrow.

I popped my head back in and called out, "Anxious, are you coming?"

The little guy lifted his chin from the striped bench seat where he was clipped in to the seatbelt catch and stared at me like I'd lost my mind. He shivered, then hunkered down and curled up with a groan.

"Fair enough," I chuckled, knowing there was no chance of him getting out until he knew we were staying put.

I shut the door and wandered over to Min who was staring at the gate with a frown. "I can't open it," she panted, her breath like clouds of smoke on the crisp air. "It's frozen solid."

"How can we camp if the gate's stuck?"

"Guess we'll have to leave Vee here and sleep in the little tent."

"No way! Are you nuts? I'm not spending Christmas Eve in a tent. We'll freeze. And how will Santa put our presents out? We need to be in Vee."

"Then you better open the gate," she giggled.

Frost sparkled on the galvanised metal, the latch stuck fast, so I pulled out my pocket knife—something I always carried with me as being a vanlifer meant I seemed to need one at least several times daily—and scraped away the ice from the latch. With a grunt, and a yank, it popped open and Min and I high-fived; we were good to go.

I hurried back to the van and trundled through, then Min closed the gate and we completed the short drive down the frozen track to a large green static caravan set up beside a very dilapidated, but rather impressive, Georgian farmhouse.

"That looks nice. On the website it said the couple who bought this place were living in the static home while they renovated the house. The campsite is ready for visitors but I think we might be the first ones. Their booking calendar was all green, no red dates where it was booked."

"You got electric hookup, didn't you?" I asked in a panic, stressing that we'd be without electricity and thus heat, and I wondered yet again if I should have bitten the bullet and got a diesel heater fitted in Vee so I wouldn't have to worry about such things.

"Of course."

After going the whole summer and well into autumn relying on solar and my large power bank for my needs, it had been a bitter pill to swallow to have to book places with an option to plug into mains power. It severely limited my choices of where I could stay, but thankfully there had been plenty of sunny days this winter so I'd still had several great and wild adventures stealth parking or staying in cheap locations, scraping by with solar and low power-consuming fairy lights strung up inside which was cosy and fun.

"They've got their work cut out for them. The roof looks sound, but the windows need replacing, and I bet it will cost a fortune to do the entire interior."

"Let's go and knock and check in. I can't wait to get set up." Min smiled at me, her nose and cheeks as red as Rudolph's, and she looked just as excited.

"You're like a little kid," I teased.

"You know I love Christmas. It's such a special time of year. And this was such a fun idea. Thanks for coming to get me. It was a long drive for you, and I appreciate it."

"It was no bother. It was time to leave Cornwall anyway. It was warmer down there, but it's bleak in the winter and I fancied getting back into the Midlands. I miss the countryside around here. So, shall we book in?"

"Let's do it." With a grin, Min exited and I joined her outside.

Building materials were piled high, bags of sand and ballast littered the site along with stacks of blocks and a battered cement mixer, which didn't exactly look ideal, but to be fair this was the middle of winter and hardly peak tourist season.

Everything was covered in ice and would be impossible to work with unless they could thaw it out. I felt a chill in my bones just thinking about working with the heavy concrete blocks and sand so hard you'd need a pick to break it up.

"Hello?" shouted Min, shivering as we approached the cabin.

"Maybe we should knock. There's smoke coming from the flue, so they're probably hunkered down inside and toasty."

"Oh, that would be nice. A fire sounds awesome."

"We could have one outside later. If I set up the gazebo beside Vee, it will trap the heat."

"Great idea. And I can do mulled wine and you can cook us a one-pot Christmas Eve wonder."

"Deal!" I grinned, looking forward to it already.

Min stepped forward and rapped on the door, then jumped back by my side as though she'd done something wrong.

"Why are you acting like you're playing knock and run?" I teased.

"I'm not. Did you ever do that? Knock on people's doors then run away and hide around the corner and giggle as they looked for who it was?"

"Me? Never," I lied, turning away so she couldn't see my face.

"Liar," she laughed, then squealed when the door was flung open.

"Hi!" said a woman of about our age with a friendly smile, wearing nothing but a pair of green shorts and a black vest. Her blond hair was incredibly straight and hung down to her backside, but her dark brown, nearly black eyes meant it was dyed, although you'd never know if it wasn't for her eye colour. With a waifish frame and a very narrow face, she was almost childlike, but short, dirty nails and muscular forearms showed she was no stranger to hard work.

"Um, hi," said Min cautiously.

"Why are you acting so cagey?" I asked, eyebrow raised. I faced the woman and said, "Hi. We booked for a few nights. We weren't sure if you were open, but the booking went through online. We hope that's alright? I'm Max, this is Min, and our dog's in the van."

"Yes, yes, come in. Sorry, we're new to this and weren't sure when you'd come, or if you'd come at all. The roads are so icy and we worried maybe you'd had an accident." Her eyes drifted to Vee and she gasped, then turned her attention back to us and asked, "Is that your VW? So cool. Sorry, of course it's yours. Duh! Anyway, I'm Maddie. Come in. Get warm while we sort out your stay."

We hurried to the door and began to take our boots off, but Maddie insisted we could leave them on as they were always in and out of the cabin because of the work they were doing, so stepped inside and she closed the door behind us.

"Wow, it's baking in here." I could feel sweat beading to the surface already and hurriedly removed my woollen hat and teased out my long brown hair, pleased I'd let it continue to grow so my ears stayed toasty for the winter. Next came my coat, then my gloves, but it was still incredibly warm. When I turned to Min, she was down to her vest and looking luscious, and I found it hard to focus on what I was meant to be doing.

"Stop gawping like that," ordered Min with a smile, knowing full well how lovely she looked.

"Sorry, I can't help it. You're so pretty."

"Aw, will you look at these two lovebirds, Roy? Isn't it sweet?"

"Sure is. Hi, I'm Roy. You must be Min, and you are?" he asked me.

"I'm Max. Sorry to disturb you. You look like you're about to go outside. Are you working on the property today? It's Christmas Eve and freezing. Surely you'll just take it easy?"

"I wish," he huffed, dragging on a grey sweater full of holes that was clearly his work attire.

"Roy has promised to only work until three, then we're going to get cosy around the fire, watch a movie, and pig out on all the food I bought. I overdid it and we have way too many biscuits, crackers, and I don't know what I was thinking about when I bought so much cheese. We'll be fat by the new year."

"We deserve it. This place has been non-stop ever since we bought it."

"We read a little on your website. Big job, is it?" I asked.

"Massive. The house is in good basic order, but I need to rebuild a few interior walls that were done badly, and it needs new wiring and central heating. It's uninhabitable, especially now with it being so cold, but we're hoping to move in by the summer when the camping season kicks in. I've been plugging away at things this winter, but it's hard. Everything takes twice as long when it's wet, and half the stuff is frozen. Maddie works even harder than me, but it will be worth it."

"It sure will. A new start. A whole new life and a great adventure. We sold up our flats in Cardiff and bought this place outright. Crazy, eh? Prices are so different in one city to another. Makes no sense."

"That sounds like fun. Running a campsite is a great business," I said, hoping they made a go of it as they seemed like nice people.

"That's what we thought. We went over the books with a fine-toothed comb and they made good money here. But the owners were getting on and wanted to retire, so we snapped it up. Anyway, sorry to babble. Let's get you booked in and I'll show you to your pitch."

"I'll do it. I'm heading out anyway," said Roy, zipping up his coat, clearly telling Maddie to get a move on as he wanted to start work. His solid build, and dark, roughly cut hair meant he looked like he was happy to slum it and was used to making do. He was clearly a man of action, unable to sit still for long.

Maddie confirmed our booking. I paid for three nights, took a longing glance at the roaring log burner, then we wrapped up in our winter clothes and followed Roy outside.

"It's not far." Roy blew on his calloused, dirty hands then slipped his gloves on. "The first thing we did when we got here a few months ago was to sort out the land and the pitches. Everything was overgrown, but it didn't take much to clear it. I cut a few branches, tidied up several areas, sorted out the wiring, and now we're good to go for guests. Shame it's out of season, but that's okay. It gives us more time to focus on the house for a few months."

"Are we the first guests?" asked Min excitedly.

"Yes, you are! And thank you for choosing us. Actually, there are a few more people expected this afternoon. I never imagined people would want to spend their Christmas at a campsite, but I guess I was wrong. Maybe they want to get away from their families."

"We thought it would be fun, and Max is a full-time vanlifer anyway," said Min, squeezing my hand.

"Great! Now, let me show you the way. It's just around the corner. You can follow me in the VW. Cool van by the way."

"Thanks."

We hurried back to Vee and I followed Roy as he took a turn on the gravel track then across the field into a hidden area off to the side, then down a little slope into a beautiful area enclosed on all sides by trees. There was a rope swing under a large oak, and I spied a stream meandering through the forest for a moment before I pulled into the pitch Roy pointed at.

"It's perfect." Min smiled at me and I grinned back.

"Sure is. What a fantastic spot. There are even fire pits to use, and picnic benches. They've done an incredible job. This place will be rammed in the summer, so we're lucky to have it to ourselves."

"Come on, let's say goodbye to Roy, then get set up." Wasting no time, Min jumped out and I followed.

I was halted immediately by a howl from the interior, so raced back and opened the door. Once unclipped, Anxious launched into my arms and began licking my face as his tail wagged wildly.

"Yes, we're here, and yes, you can go and play. Don't go far, and say hello to Roy first."

Anxious' head snapped around, keen to meet a new friend, then wriggled like a fish in a sock—um, don't know where that analogy came from! I have never, and would never, recommend putting fish in socks—as he spotted Roy.

"Hey there, little fella," laughed Roy as he stroked the wriggly Jack Russell who slid like the aforementioned fish into Roy's arms and flipped upside down for a tummy rub.

"He likes you," laughed Min, shaking her head at his antics.

"I think you might be right. Here you go, boy." Roy lowered Anxious, who shook himself out then trotted off for a pee and to explore.

"Will this pitch be okay? You can go anywhere, but I think this is the best one, and as you're our first guests you get to christen it."

"It's perfect. Oh, Roy, thank you so much. It's a special place, I can tell."

"It really is. Thanks for this. It will be nice to wake up on Christmas morning in such a stunning location."

"There's a stack of firewood under that tarp there, but if you need more grab some from the barn up by the house.

We have loads. Are you sure you'll be okay out here for Christmas? Will you be warm enough in the van?"

"We have a heater, and an absolute ton of food. We went shopping earlier and have all we need," I explained.

"Then enjoy. Remember, if you need anything, just holler." Roy smiled, then left to continue his renovations.

Wasting no time, and laughing like schoolchildren, we merrily set up the gazebo, unpacked Vee so I could arrange the outside kitchen, having found that no matter the weather, cooking outdoors was always preferable to the cramped conditions inside. Having space to move about freely beat the warmth factor every time, so I got everything organised, kept the sides of the gazebo zipped up, but we erected it so that we could step from Vee into the shelter without getting wet if it rained.

Once done, we hauled the fire bowl, a large steel box open on the front and on legs, over to a safe distance from anything combustible and I lit a fire then erected the windbreaks around our new camp so we'd be as snug as possible given the circumstances. The difference was noticeable instantly, and with happy grins we settled in the camping chairs around the fire and sipped on hot chocolate with loads of marshmallows, about as content as two people could be sitting in a field in minus two on Christmas Eve.

It wasn't long before another vehicle arrived. A single man exited a Ford Transit Custom that was very well kitted-out by the glance I got as he opened up. He waved cheerily and shouted hello, then set up a tent that hitched over the roof to give him extra space and privacy. He stayed in his pitch, but we could hear him banging about on occasion.

"We should get one to fit over Vee. It would make it really roomy," said Min.

"Maybe, but I've got used to the gazebo now. It's more versatile. You can leave it behind when you want to go somewhere."

"True. But you can get driveway awnings now that you park right next to. Like that man's tent, I suppose. Look, here's someone else. And another van behind them. Wow, this place is busy. I didn't think anyone else would come today."

"I guess some people are either alone for Christmas or want to escape the in-laws," I laughed.

"You could be right," giggled Min, stroking Anxious as he snored in her lap.

There's nothing more fun than watching how others set up for camping or seeing what they do with their vans, so we watched a couple in their sixties skid to a stop, jump out, then rush around pulling out an awning on their old motorhome then hurry back inside and turn the TV on so loud it blared until we heard the woman shout and the man turned it down.

The other van was an impressive motorhome from the early two thousands with all the extras. Rhino roof rack, huge retractable awning, bike rack on the rear, spoilers, tinted windows, chrome running board and matching trim, and no doubt with an interior that looked like it was fresh from a factory refurb. Surprisingly, the owner was a man I guessed to be in his early forties. He seemed harried, and with all the layers, and repeatedly called out loudly to his children and wife we were yet to see. After a few minutes of dashing about while noise rose from inside, their camp was complete with the awning out, chairs arranged, and a table set up.

The man shouted a hello but was clearly busy with things inside the motorhome and that was the last we saw of them.

After a long and enjoyable walk through the surrounding countryside, we returned and settled down with mulled wine and a roaring fire before I put dinner on. It was a lovely chilled evening with us chatting, and drinking Prosecco after the mulled wine, but as I turned on the fairy lights we'd strung up around the gazebo and the other campers retired to their vehicles, it became truly special once we were alone outside.

Huddled close with a blanket around our shoulders, the fire blazing, our cheeks rosy as we had on all the clothes, it felt magical as ice crystals formed on the grass and darkness slammed in like the sun couldn't wait to get some rest.

"This has been so much fun," murmured Min. "Thank you."

"Thank you for coming. It's going to be a Christmas like no other. Don't forget, we promised no presents."

"I remember. Good food and great company are all I want this year."

"Let's get inside. I put the heater on and we can watch a movie on my laptop. Something Christmassy."

"Sounds lovely."

After sorting out the fire and stowing the chairs, we retreated into the warmth and settled beneath the blankets on the rock n roll bed I'd actually remembered to sort out earlier, with a glass of wine in hand and a funny festive movie. Elf never got old, and we laughed until it was over then curled up and I switched the lights off.

"See you on Christmas day." I leaned over, and it wasn't very far, and kissed Min's cheek.

"See you tomorrow. Is it silly that I'm excited? I know it's just another day, but it always feels special. Especially with us spending it together."

"Every day is special when we're together." I turned to smile at her, but Min was already fast asleep.

I kissed Anxious' head and he snuffled in his sleep, then I curled up next to the two souls I loved more than anything in the world and drifted off for a perfect night's sleep.

Chapter 2

"Blimey, it's absolutely freezing," I gasped as my eyes snapped open and I lamented not leaving the heater on overnight; paranoia about safety wouldn't let me. My breath formed a dense cloud as I shivered but nevertheless pulled back the covers to get up.

"Hey, don't do that!" Min grabbed the duvet and yanked it up to her chin, pulling me back down with it. "Wow, it's so cold. Oh no, now I really need a pee. Like, right now."

"Then you better get up," I laughed, in desperate need of relief myself. "Merry Christmas."

"Merry Christmas. We're going to have a fantastic day. I just know it. Lovely walks, lots of great food, a drink at lunchtime, and nothing to do but relax. I'm so looking forward to it."

"Me too."

"Right, wish me luck. Um, where's Anxious?"

I lifted the duvet and winked at Min as I revealed the little guy halfway down the bed, eyes squeezed shut, still as a rock.

"He's still asleep?"

"He's pretending to be because he doesn't want to get up," I giggled, tickling his tummy. Unable to resist, his tail wagged and he reluctantly opened an eye then shut it again hastily.

"Silly boy. Come on, Anxious, you must need a wee too." Min folded back the bedding and Anxious whined but dutifully belly crawled up to the pillows then stretched out before wagging happily.

"You little sneak! Now we're all up. Merry Christmas, Anxious."

Min wished him a happy Christmas, too, and we cuddled him, both grinning, our mood buoyant, as this promised to be a fun and very different to normal day. But first, we had to make the dreaded morning dash.

Still in our jim-jams, we draped blankets over our shoulders and I switched on the heater. We arranged the bedding, and I set the rock n roll bed back into its bench seat position to give us some room, then turned to find Min frowning with her hands on her hips.

"What's wrong?"

"I thought we said no presents? Max, how could you? Now I feel awful as I didn't get you anything."

"I didn't get you anything either," I said, confused.

"No, then how do you explain this?" Min stepped aside and leaned back against the tiny kitchen counter to reveal a stack of presents in red and white wrapping paper. There were just about all the bows and tinsel on the pile of gifts, and on the counter beside Min was a small tree festooned with more tinsel and mini baubles of purple and gold, and even lights plugged in and flashing. I hadn't even noticed as my back had been turned and I was busy with the bed, but it looked incredible.

"Yes, very funny," I laughed. "The tree looks great, and I love the tinsel, but why did you do this, Min? We promised."

"Hey, don't you try to turn this around on me. I didn't do it. This was you."

"You promise you didn't set this up in the night?"

"Of course not! And do you promise?"

"I swear it wasn't me. We made an agreement. We should have done a tree, though, but it wasn't me."

"Wow! Oh, gosh, and look, the mince pie has been half eaten, the carrot's been nibbled, and the milk is nearly gone."

"So Santa really has been?" I asked, incredulous. Then I sniggered, as Min nearly fooled me, but when I studied her I realised she had the same look I knew I had.

"You still think it was me, don't you?" I asked.

"Of course. And you believe it was me, don't you?"

"It has to be you. Do you promise you didn't do any of this? Not even eating the mince pie?"

"I swear. And it wasn't Anxious as no way would he leave half a mince pie. He loves them. That's why we put it up on the shelf. Max, what is going on here?"

"I guess Santa actually came." I shrugged, unable to come up with another explanation.

"Don't be silly. He only comes for children, not adults in their thirties in VWs. Max, what is going on?"

"I honestly don't know. It must be Santa," I insisted.

Min shook her head playfully, sending her golden locks cascading onto her shoulders and framing her beautiful face perfectly. "No way."

"You look so pretty in the morning. Tousled and sleepy. You smell nice too." I stepped forward for a sniff, but she backed away with her hands up.

"You and your sniffing. It's weird," she teased, eyes dancing with mirth, the blue sparkling as it caught the flashing lights on the tree.

"It's not. It's normal. Now, let's get to the loos. I really need to go."

"Me too." Min crossed her legs and nodded vigorously.

Anxious whimpered as he pawed at the door. He was desperate, too, and would have no qualms about going if he had to.

Min grabbed the handle and went to open the door, but for some reason she'd changed her mind and simply gripped it tight but didn't open it.

"Hurry up!"

"I'm trying. It's stuck."

"It never gets stuck. It slides, so how can it be?"

"I don't know, but I'm telling you it won't budge." Min grunted as she tugged at the handle, her body angled to the left to get more weight behind her pull, but nothing happened. "It's not working. Maybe it's frozen solid."

"Let me try."

We swapped positions and I yanked hard, but she was right and it refused to move. Wondering what the deal was, I cupped my hands and pressed my face to the frosty window to look outside, then shook my head and laughed softly.

"What's so funny? Max, I'm desperate. I'm going to try the passenger door."

"I wouldn't bother if I were you. That will be even harder. I think we'll have to go through the window."

"Why wouldn't the other door work? What are you talking about?"

I took a step back and guided Min to the window, then suggested, "Take a look outside. Not that there's much to see."

Frowning, she nevertheless peered out, then gasped, "No way. Snow! And lots of it."

"I'm guessing it came down heavy in the night and there must have been a lot of wind. We've got snowdrifts right up to the roof in places, so, er, we're trapped. Looks like the gazebo's had it because of the weight."

"We can't be stuck! I need to pee. So do you, and so does Anxious."

Anxious whined in agreement and began hopping around. Things were getting serious.

"Let me see if I can unwind the window. Hopefully, it isn't frozen." I moved into the front, then shuffled into the passenger seat and tried the handle; it turned easily enough. What I hadn't anticipated was the volume of snow that tumbled into the van and covered my lap. I was frozen and soaked in an instant.

"Careful! You'll fill the van with it."

"It's not quite that bad, but it is pretty bad." I wound the window all the way down, getting covered in more snow, then scooped the seemingly impenetrable wall of white away with my hands until beautiful daylight shone through.

With a grin of resignation, and a nod to Min, who returned the gesture, I faced the driver's seat then squatted and reached outside to grip the roof. Fingers already numb, I heaved myself out until I was sitting on the door frame, then awkwardly crawled up so I could get my legs out. Pushing with my feet, and with snow falling down the back of my pyjamas giving me a numb bum, I found myself on the roof.

"Max, are you okay?" Min called, her head poking through the window.

"Fine. Pass Anxious out. He's gonna pee inside otherwise."

"Then me. I'm bursting." Min passed the whining pooch out and I placed him on the roof, but he sank and was buried before I hauled him out, then brushed the thick snow aside and settled him. He trotted to the edge, then cocked a leg and did the necessary with a groan of relief. On and on it went, the steam rising, Anxious making yellow snow over the side.

Min reached out, so I helped her onto the roof and there we stood in our pyjamas, nothing but our thick socks, now soaked and totally not warm, and slippers on our feet, shivering in the crisp morning on Christmas Day, marooned on the roof of our van with a white winter wonderland all around. The sky was blue, not a cloud in sight, the snow dazzling, but it was absolutely freezing and my guess was it must have easily been minus five if not lower.

"What now?" asked Min.

"We jump." I gripped Min's hand and grinned, then asked, "Ready?" as I scooped up Anxious with my free hand.

"You can't be serious? We'll be buried."

"Not if we jump past the snowdrift. It's up against the van, but we can get past it. It looks deep enough to give us a soft landing, but we can stand in it. Here we go."

"No, not yet!"

But I ignored her, and jumped, dragging Min with me, and we landed with a soft thud on our backsides, buried to our waists. Releasing Min, I floundered until I managed to get to my feet, the snow actually halfway up my shins. Reaching out, I heaved and got Min to stand, but her shorter stature meant it was almost up to her knees and she nearly toppled back over.

"Where's Anxious?" she gasped, shivering.

"I don't know. I let go so I could stand."

Right on cue, the rather perplexed dog bounded out of the snow beside us and landed on top of it, his light weight meaning he could stand there for a few seconds before he sank. Stifling a laugh, I picked him up and held him close so he could warm up, and tried not to think about how cold I was already.

"Let's get away from the snowdrift so we can check this out." I reached out and took Min's willing hand, then we cautiously tried to move. It wasn't easy as each step entailed lifting your legs up very high to escape the snow then pulling the trailing one from behind. The going was incredibly slow and exhausting, but we managed to get some space then both stopped, breathing heavily, our breath visible.

"Wow! Will you look at that? How crazy is this? Max, it snowed for Christmas! It never does this. How awesome." Min smiled, then kissed my cheek, excited to finally have a white Christmas.

"It looks incredible, and I'm amazed how thick the covering is. With it being so cold, it's bound to last for days unless it rains, and I doubt it will. If it freezes, we'll be in trouble, as the windows and doors will seize up, so we should shift as much as we can from Vee. Maybe Maddie and Roy will lend us a snow shovel. The gazebo's definitely had it, though, and I can't even see the table or the rest of the kitchen stuff."

"First we need to get dressed, then we need to put our wellies on and clean socks and underwear. I'm not spending Christmas Day in dirty knickers."

"The very thought makes me shudder," I teased, keeping quiet about my lack of hygiene now and then when I was on the road. Two days once in a while is fine for your boxers, right?

Min put her arm around my waist and huddled close for warmth, and I placed my arm around her shoulder. "Merry Christmas, love. This is going to be a very special day. I can feel it. Santa's been, we have a tree, there's real snow, and we get to open lots of presents. Are you sure it wasn't you?"

"Max, it really wasn't. Let's just enjoy the day. We can have snowball fights too."

"Right now?"

"No. Right now I have to go use the facilities."

We faced the smart new building that housed toilets, showers, several sinks to wash the dishes, and shiny refuse bins, then steeled ourselves for an arduous walk through the snow that had drifted in many places and would make the going tough indeed.

With no other choice, we made our way over, fighting the snow that got everywhere. By the time we reached the safety of the building, my toes were numb and my slippers were frozen solid. Under the overhang of the roof the ground was clear, so we hurried into the appropriate rooms and our sighs were so loud each of us could hear the other.

We regrouped outside with Anxious waiting, head cocked, glancing from us to the snow, eyes alight with excitement.

"Someone wants to play," noted Min.

"He sure does," I laughed. "But first we have to get dressed and put some layers on. I'm frozen. We should leave the heater on, too, or everything in the van will freeze solid if it hasn't already. I could do with a few cups of coffee too."

"Deal. We'll dress, drink, sort out the stuff outside, then play. Oh, Max, isn't this wonderful? It couldn't feel more like Christmas unless there was a snowman."

I nodded in agreement as I surveyed the enclosed piece of land we were staying in, admiring the snow weighing the branches of the trees down, how the other vehicles were half buried by the drifts but not as extreme as ours, presumably because of the wind direction, but as my gaze travelled from one vehicle to the next, I paused and gasped.

"I think Santa must have known what you'd wish for today and has granted that wish." I nodded to the centre of the campsite and when Min followed the direction her eyes went wide in shock and delight and she gasped.

"A snowman! Someone made a snowman! It's huge. Bigger than a person. It's only eight in the morning and not even properly light yet, so when did they do this?"

"I have no idea. Let's go investigate. He's got a scarf on and a hat, but I can't make out the rest properly."

Grinning from ear to ear, and feeling about as festive as it was possible to be, we waded through the snow slowly, with Anxious refusing to be carried and bounding along in our footsteps, whining when he got stuck and needed to be rescued.

We made it eventually, shivering but happy, and stood before the towering snowman, easily seven feet tall.

"It's very impressive. Black stones for eyes and to make the mouth shape, a beat-up flat cap, and even a scarf. I love the arms made from twigs. He even has stones to look like jacket buttons. This is a proper snowman." Min reached out and stroked the curve of the body, then smiled. "We'll have to make one, too, then he can have a friend."

"Good idea, but not without wearing gloves and some decent clothes. It's weird, but everyone else is still in their vehicles, with no sign they've been out, so who did this?"

"There's a new motorhome tucked away over there, so maybe it was them. Look, there are footprints around it, so I bet it was them."

"I didn't see it over there," I admitted, having completely overlooked the large vehicle half-hidden by the trees. But Min was right and there were signs of activity around it and snow had been shifted from the doors so the occupants could get in and out easily. "They must have come after we went in for the night. Bit weird to make a snowman in the dark early in the morning though. They're keen."

"I bet they have kids with them and they were so excited it had snowed that they couldn't wait."

Anxious popped up from a deep patch and sat, head cocked, staring at the snowman. He began to growl.

"It's okay," soothed Min. "It's just a snowman, Anxious. A pretend person made of snow. Don't be scared." She winked at me, face flushed with mirth and festive cheer, but her smile faded as Anxious barked.

"Ssh," I hissed. "You'll wake everyone up. Quiet, Anxious."

My best buddy barked loudly, the sound muted by the snow but still a piercing cry, then he lunged forward, growling wildly, tail down, ears pinned to his head, his distress obvious.

I stumbled forward to get him before he woke the entire campsite, but he sidestepped just as I reached to grab him and bounded over then began pawing at the base of the poor snowman.

"Anxious, whatever has got into you?" demanded Min as she tried to race forward but fell flat on her face.

I tried to hide my snigger but failed, so, laughing, I helped her stand then brushed the snow from her shoulders, aching to pat down her chest but thinking better of it, then our eyes met and she grinned, clearly reading my mind.

"I can finish the rest, thanks," she said with a wink.

Our mirth was short-lived as Anxious was going spare yipping and scratching at the snowman, so I scrambled over and finally managed to pick him up. Turning the little guy to face me, his legs still working hard in mid-air, I asked, "What's wrong? Why are you so against snowmen? You always loved the snow when we got it. I know we never had it like this, but it's just a pretend person. It isn't real."

Anxious listened dutifully, and calmed, so I spun him around as Min sidled up beside us, and we looked at the cool figure before us. A stone button fell off the mouth, making it lopsided, and this was all the impetus Anxious needed. He wriggled frantically, then launched out of my arms at the head and crashed into it.

"Anxious, no!" shouted Min, then snatched out a hand and pulled him off as the head began to wobble.

We stood back and watched as the poor snowman's head teetered, then the thin dense ice connecting it to the body cracked and it toppled sideways.

Anxious turned to us, smiling, tail wagging, as if to say, "See, I warned you."

Min and I stared in horror at what was revealed. In place of the snowman's head was the real head of a man. His face was frozen solid in a terrifying grimace, his eyes open and staring lifelessly. His dark bushy beard shone with ice as the sun bounced off it, the skin was almost blue, and his short brown hair was stiff and covered in snow and ice.

"Merry Christmas," I sighed, and hugged Min as she buried her face in my chest.

Doors to motorhomes and campervans opened if they could, whilst voices could be heard from inside others, complaining about being stuck.

And so began the Christmas corpse mystery.

At least we had presents to unwrap.

Chapter 3

"It's okay," I soothed. "He's dead."

Min pulled back and looked into my eyes with a frown. "I know that! It doesn't make me feel better. Those are your words of hope?"

"Was I meant to say words of hope? Sorry, I'm not sure what I should say. Are you alright? I know it's a shock." I glanced past Min to the snowman and the corpse staring back at me, and shuddered.

"I'm okay, I guess. Max, this is awful. It's Christmas and that poor man is dead. He is dead, isn't he?" Min released me and turned cautiously to stare at the awful sight. "Yeah, he's dead. Should we check anyway? And what do we do now?"

"Now we have to call the police and warn our neighbours. Either it was one of them, or our hosts, or there's a snowman-building maniac on the loose and for some reason they trudged all the way here to build it around the dead guy."

"Who does that? What's the point? How did they even get the body here? Did they drag him through the snow then build around him? Max, that's so much effort." Min cuddled in to me again after turning away, but she made several good points.

"It's a real mystery, for sure, and whoever did this was certainly determined to complete their snowman. I mean, he even has a hat and a scarf."

"I bet they're from the dead man. Assuming the rest of him is in there. Maybe it's just a head like that case you dealt with at the comedy festival."

"Maybe, but I don't think so. You can see a little of his chest."

Min gasped, and asked, "You mean he's naked?"

"I didn't look closely. Maybe we should?"

Min nodded, then released her tight hold on me and together we faced the snowman.

Anxious glanced over his shoulder then wagged as we approached. Our teeth chattered, and I knew we only had a few minutes before we'd have to get into the warm and change out of our frozen and soaked clothes or we'd be losing fingers and toes, maybe a nose and ear too.

Min whistled and Anxious attempted to run to her, then stopped and shook himself out when he realised it was an exercise in futility. The snow was simply too deep and all he did was sink; even when he craned his neck only his nose was visible.

Taking pity on the poor guy, Min scooped him up and held him tight to her chest. "He's freezing. He's got icicles stuck in his fur. We need to get him inside soon or he'll be like the poor snowman."

"We should check on the body, then we'll go in. Won't be long."

"Max, look, you can see where he was dragged. There's a depression in the snow leading back around to the main field."

"You're right! So, we know he must have been pulled along, maybe on a sledge judging by the track. Looks like the marks those plastic curved ones make, not ones on runners. Or a tarp, possibly."

"Who would have a sledge handy? And why come here to do this? It has to be personal, right?"

"That's what I was thinking," I admitted. "Whoever did this must have been making a point. They must have driven as close as they could, unloaded the body, dragged him here, then built the snowman around him. That's a lot of trouble and a huge risk. Anyone could have seen. Did you hear anything last night?"

"Nothing. Even though I was excited about Christmas, I was out until this morning. This makes no sense. They could have been spotted, or anything could have happened. Think they drove into the field? Wouldn't Maddie and Roy have heard?"

"Maybe, but maybe not. If they were asleep like everyone else, they wouldn't have heard. Unless…" I left the thought dangling, but Min nodded; we were both thinking the same thing.

"Unless Maddie and Roy are the killers."

"It's possible, but they seemed nice, and why on earth would they dump a corpse on their own land like this? They want to make a go of the business, not ruin it before it even gets started. Who else is here?"

"The man in the Transit with the tent attached, the couple with the old van and the loud TV, and the family with the children. Plus, the mystery van that arrived after we were inside. We didn't even hear them arrive either."

We studied the mystery motorhome, a large vehicle with rental stickers, but who were they, and why arrive so late? Setting up in the dark is never fun, but I suppose all they'd done was park, but I was surprised we hadn't seen their lights or heard them.

Min frowned as she gnawed at her lip like she always did when nervous or thinking. Seemingly resolute, she said, "We need to check the tracks around the vehicles to see if anyone's been outside yet."

"You're right, so we should go and do that now. Maybe trace the route the killer took too. First, let's take a look at him, but let's not disturb anything as the police will want to check everything over."

"Okay, but let's be quick. I can't feel my toes. We're in slippers and this is getting dangerous. We could get frostbite."

"Deal."

Screams and squeals rang out from the family motorhome; the kids were clearly up and excited. A young child was screeching with delight and shouting out about Santa and Rudolph as we approached the snowman. It was a strange way to inspect a corpse, but we did it anyway. The man's beard was now covered in ice crystals after being exposed to the air, and his skin had turned even more blue.

He wore a simple silver belcher chain just visible at the neck line along with the collar of a red and black thick chequered shirt, but seemingly no coat. The rest of his body was still covered in the densely packed snow, so there was no way of telling if he was intact or what was going on underneath, and we knew better than to disturb anything.

Next, we inspected the areas around the various vehicles without straying too far from our position. From what we could tell, the ground was undisturbed around all but the new one. Almost imperceptible footprints because of continuing snow led from the vehicle over to first one van then to ours, and to the snowman. Was it that simple? They'd arrived, then carried the man over and built around him? Why go to the other vehicle then ours?

What about the drag marks across the field? We fought the snow and got closer to the large rental then stopped a decent distance away for fear of disturbing what might be vital evidence, and there was no doubt that whoever was inside had been back and forth several times to the motorhome from our van and the snowman and the family vehicle. They'd tried to walk in their own footprints to avoid the worst of the snow, but failed and had trodden the ground until it was compact in places but with a fresh covering of fluffy powder over it, almost hiding the prints entirely. It was as we'd thought earlier and they'd spent some time clearing away the drifts from the motorhome so they could get in and out easily.

"Can it be this easy?" Min shivered as she grasped my arm and dragged my hand from my side then clutched it tight. "Is whoever's inside the killer or killers?"

"It's pretty dumb if that's true. They haven't even tried to hide their movements. Why stay if they did it? Makes no sense. I think we need to call the police."

"Shouldn't we warn Maddie and Roy first? Maybe check they're okay? What if they're dead?" Min squeezed tight, eyes darting back towards the main field and the house beyond.

"Maybe we should warn them. But what if they did it?"

"They were so sweet and helpful. No way would they do this."

"You're right, but first we need to get changed. We should warn everyone here. People might be in danger. We need to make sure everyone's alive and well. Not what anyone wants to deal with on Christmas Day, but we have no choice."

"Agreed. Can we please get changed first? I can't stay out her another minute."

"Sure. I doubt anyone else will come outside yet. It's early, and when they do try to get out they'll have to clear the snow. They're probably all stuck inside like we were apart from in the rental. Come on, let's get dressed."

We hurried as best we could back to Vee, where we had to scoop away the snow with frozen hands to reveal the door. After five minutes we were shattered, beyond cold, and yet sweating at the same time. I couldn't feel my feet at all now and Min looked ready to collapse.

The moment the door slid open, Anxious shot inside and launched onto the bench seat then shook from head to tail, sending snow and ice everywhere. We hurried inside, I closed the door, and Min turned the heater on to full. As we stripped down, Min's insistence on dressing and undressing with her back turned forgotten in her haste to shed her stiff PJs, I couldn't stop myself from taking a sneaky peek. I gasped, and not from the cold, as seeing her naked for the first time in so long brought back so many memories and reminded me how beautiful she was both inside and out, but then she slid on her clothes and I was left standing there, stark naked, trying to focus on what I was supposed to be doing.

"Get dressed!" she hissed, eyes trailing down from my face. "Your legs are blue and your feet are almost black with cold. Hurry, Max, get dressed."

I caught the gasp as she glanced at my body, and grinned despite the situation. "Yes, ma'am." I winked, then slid on underwear, thick socks, jeans, a vest, then a T-shirt, followed by a Christmas jumper with a picture of Rudolph, and felt the difference immediately.

In the cramped space we were right on top of each other as we battled with sweaters and scarves and tried to give each other a little room, but the reality was that dressing in a small van was far from ideal and the limited space was a reminder that not everything about vanlife was perfect.

Min set the kettle to boil while I steeled myself for what I had to do, then I put on my boots and hurriedly went outside to the rear and opened up to retrieve our wellies from the storage area and dashed back inside, thankful for the layers, the difference from earlier welcome.

With the door closed and the heat enveloping me, and with Min smiling in thanks, I settled next to Anxious and rubbed him with his towel until he was dry, then wrapped him up in a fresh one. He groaned happily and curled up with the towel draped over him so only his head was seen, and watched as Min made coffee and I wondered about the tree and gifts. Had Santa really been? I laughed at the thought, but how were the presents here? Min swore it wasn't her, but was she just teasing?

She caught me staring and asked, "You're thinking it was me, aren't you? Well, I'm thinking it was you. It has to be. Do you swear it wasn't?"

"I do. Do you?"

"Yes, I swear. Max, this means someone came in while we were sleeping. What could the presents be? Is it a trick by the killer? Body parts maybe?" Min shuddered as her eyes widened.

"Maybe we'll leave the unwrapping until later," I suggested. "We need to deal with more important things."

"Like dinner?" Min snorted a nervous laugh before slapping a hand over her mouth and blurting, "I'm so sorry, that was in bad taste. It's the nerves. Um, but we will have dinner, right?"

"Of course we will. Let's get the rest of our gear on then try to sort this mess out. First, we should visit the other guests, then tell our hosts, then call the police."

"Shouldn't we call the police first? Just so we know they're coming?"

"Maybe you're right. Yes, I'll do that." The call was quick, and I was told to be careful and someone would arrive as soon as possible, but with the snow it might be a while as many roads were impassable. I hadn't even considered access, but the chances were high that the road to the campsite was a no-go. If that was the case, how had the killer arrived then left? More questions without answers.

We hastily gulped our coffee then donned coats, hats, and gloves, and slipped our wellies on at the doorway, having to take turns because of the lack of space. We finished our drinks, the bitter warmth as the liquid hit my empty stomach comforting, then with a nod to each other I slid the door open and we stepped out into a true winter wonderland.

The snow was coming down so thick that visibility was almost at zero. We pulled our hats low to our eyes, wrapped our scarves over our mouths, then turned to get Anxious.

He looked at us with imploring eyes, snuggled up on the bench seat beneath his towel, so with a muffled agreement we told him he could stay inside.

Securing him in the warmth, I closed the door and we faced the snowstorm. There's always something magical about snow. The world goes silent, sound vanquished, and we stood for a moment enjoying the quiet, watching as thick snowflakes drifted down. The sky was now white, the sun gone, the snow falling faster and faster, so dense I could hardly even see Min right beside me.

I pointed to the van occupied by the lone man. Min nodded in agreement, so we approached as he was closest and directly opposite us. I led the way so Min could follow in my footsteps, but the going was tough and getting harder by the second as all signs of any precious movement on the campsite were rapidly obliterated under a covering of fresh snow. Finally, we made it to the Transit, but with his attached tent there was nothing to knock on but the fabric so rather than just unzip it and walk inside, I lowered my scarf and shouted, "Hello?"

A moment later I heard the side door slide open then shut and the zip to the tent was opened, revealing a man of roughly forty looking about as haggard as anyone I'd ever seen on a campsite. The smell of sour whisky was so strong I had to take a step back, but then I caught a whiff of his body odour and knew this guy had been on the road for a while and hadn't had a shower any time lately. He was either a vanlifer or had been on holiday for a while, and judging by the amount of gear and his setup, I was certain spent more time in his van than anywhere else.

"Hey," he mumbled, rubbing at his red face and scalp, the hair down to the bone, but with a long beard sticking out sideways like he'd just rolled out of bed.

"Hi. Sorry to disturb you, especially on Christmas, but we need to talk."

"I wasn't making any trouble!" he said hurriedly. "I always keep the noise down. I was just getting things ready for breakfast."

"No, sorry, I didn't mean you were noisy. Of course you weren't. Merry Christmas by the way."

"Um, yeah, back at you. Just another day, really. They blend into one."

Min stepped forward and asked, "Are you a vanlifer? Max here is. I'm Min, his, um, friend."

"Friend?" I asked, eyebrow raised and a smirk spreading.

"Yes, friend," she snapped, daring me to go into detail.

"Ah, a fellow traveller. I'm Kev. Been a few years for me now. Always on the road, travelling about, but the last few days have been rough. I got some bad news and hit the bottle hard last night. Sorry if I stink, but I haven't had time to…" Kev's words died on his breath as he poked his head out of the tent and whistled. "Blimey! Look at that. Snow. And lots of it. Cool. We never normally get it when we want it most. Can't beat snow on Christmas Day. So cool. Man, it's deep too. You guys must be freezing. Wanna come in?" Kev stepped aside, revealing his tent space that was extremely well-organised and made me gasp as I did like a neat environment.

He had a smart kitchen setup in the tent on a long table, with a chair and a small table in the centre and a nice outdoor rug covering most of the groundsheet. Heat billowed from the open door of his van, the interior clearly done professionally and to a very high standard from what little I could see. All his gear was top-of-the-range, matching the accessories he'd added to his Transit Custom.

"We won't come in, but thank you," said Min. "You have some nice equipment."

"Gotta get the best," he said, brightening. "I do get carried away at times, and I spent a fortune on the van, but hey, it's my home and it's still way cheaper than running a large house. So, to what do I owe the pleasure?" Kev waited expectantly, then his eyes drifted to the snow, a smile spreading. Snow does that to everyone. You can't help but feel happier. Sometimes it means a day off work or school, other times it means you get to go out and fool around.

"There's a dead man stuck inside a snowman. Someone built it around him. We were wondering if you killed him." Min leaned forward, squinted, and glared at him, vibing him to confess.

"Oh, yeah, course. Right, you got me fair and square. I killed him. Sorry to pretend I didn't know it was snowing. You better call the cops, I guess." Kev put his hands out like we could cuff him and hung his head.

All I could think was, "Blimey, that got solved easily."

Then Kev lunged.

Chapter 4

He grabbed my jacket and pulled me close then laughed. The whisky smell was almost too much for me and I turned my head aside as he said, "Very funny, guys. What a pair of jokers. Bit weird disturbing someone on Christmas Day to play such a dumb practical joke, isn't it?"

Sighing with relief, and deflating, Min asked, "So you didn't kill him?"

"Are you being serious?"

"I'm afraid we are. We weren't fooling," I explained. "We found him just now. We had to use the facilities and our dog knocked the snowman's head off and we found the dead guy in there. Someone mostly likely dragged him there and built it around him."

"In the middle of the night, in the dark, with all these people here? Why would anyone do that? What's the point? Look, sorry, but I'm feeling hungover and aren't sure if this is a wind-up or not."

"It's no joke, we promise," I assured him. "It's real. We're giving everyone a heads up. I've called the police and —"

"The cops are coming!" Kev scratched at his beard manically, rubbing it raw, and despite the freezing conditions and the fact he was wearing jeans and a T-shirt as he was clearly toasty in his van, he began to sweat.

"Yes. Is that a problem?" asked Min, nudging me in a less than subtle way.

"Suppose not. Me and the coppers don't get along. I have history. It's why I chose vanlife. Less bother from anyone, and I finally got away from the bad influences in my life. Apart from the booze. That follows me around wherever I go," he admitted, eyes downcast.

"We don't judge. We take people as we find them," I said, smiling and nodding.

"Max, that means a lot. Truly. It's not often anyone's so understanding. Just so you don't wonder, I got done for GBH. I beat the crap out of a guy who was dealing drugs to kids on the corner where I used to live, and got into serious trouble for it. I'd had enough, so did what I did, but I can never go back. That old life is gone now, and I don't regret belting the guy, only that I had to go to prison. We good?"

"We're good."

"Absolutely," said Min, reaching out and squeezing his arm, his faded tattoos making strange shapes as she did so.

"Thanks, guys, you're the best. So, what should I do? Want any help?"

"No thanks. We're just doing the rounds telling everyone, but please stay aware and wait for the police."

"Man, they'll be all over me because of this. What a headache."

"If you didn't do it, you'll be fine. And we don't think you did, right, Min?"

"No way. You're a nice man, so simply tell the truth and you'll be fine."

"Thanks. Okay, I'm gonna have a coffee. See you later, I guess." With a shrug, Kev zipped up the tent then closed the van door and got about his solo Christmas morning.

It made me acutely aware how lucky I was to have Min with me on this day. If she wasn't here, I could have gone to my folks' house and had company and as much love as I could stand. But for many, the holidays were a very lonely time of year, and it played havoc with their mental health. Sometimes it's easy to overlook how privileged you are, and it has nothing to do with money, but all to do with love. Family, friends, companionship, you couldn't put a price on such things and this was a timely reminder that I was the luckiest guy on earth.

"What now?" I wondered.

"We tell the others, and we have to check on Maddie and Roy." Min's jaw was set firm, an unmistakable determined look on her face I knew only too well.

"You've already decided we're going to try and solve this, haven't you?"

With a frown, she asked, "Of course. Haven't you? Max, you always get to solve the crimes, but this time I'm here from the start and I'm going to help."

"You don't want to leave it for the police and just enjoy Christmas?"

"Of course I want to enjoy Christmas. Look at it. It's awesome out here. We even have presents and a tree. Although, that is still rather worrying. Would the killer sneak in and out of Vee and leave us gifts? What if they left something nasty in them? A bomb, maybe?" Min's eyes were two saucers as she glanced back at our home.

"I doubt the killer wants to blow us up," I chuckled. "Although, it is a real mystery. Come on, let's go and tell everyone, then head up to the house."

With a nod, Min linked her arm through mine and we battled the snow, my feet already freezing despite thick socks and my wellies. My face tingled, and I knew my cheeks were as rosy as Min's and my nose was most likely purple if it was anything like the love of my life's. Strangely, I felt happy, and that was a concern.

Obviously, it was because I was here with the woman I adored, and had let slip through my fingers while I obsessed over work and failed to pay her the attention she deserved. Now divorced for over a year and a half, we were closer than ever, and I'd ditched my old ways and proved to myself and her that I was not that man, and knew how awful I'd been. Min wanted to wait until the next summer for us to get back together, but we'd been spending more and more time with each other the last few months since I became a vanlifer, and there was now no doubt in my mind that we would be a couple again, and for life this time.

She might have divorced me, and I definitely deserved it, but I had done all in my power to make amends, and was a better person for it.

So despite the terrible situation, I was happy, because she was here. And I had to admit that trying to solve this crime with her would be fun, in a worrying way, but it was churlish to try to deny the excitement and the chance to use my brain to figure this out.

The obvious questions were, who was the deceased, and why had the killer gone to such lengths to stage the corpse like this? This was no random killing; it was personal. It had to be. And it had to be linked to the campsite. Meaning, to Maddie and Roy, as it was all done on their land. But why? In time, we'd figure this out.

"I know what you're thinking," teased Min, a wicked glint in her eye.

"And I know what you're thinking," I laughed, pulling her in tighter. "You look excited, and you really want to catch the killer. Yes, it's sad, and we both feel bad for getting a buzz out of this, but if we can help clear this up, it's a good thing, so we shouldn't be too harsh on ourselves."

"Max, that's exactly it! But I do feel terrible for being excited. A man is dead, and that's atrocious, yet I can't help getting worked up about it as we have a true festive mystery on our hands."

"All the detectives I've spoken to seem to feel the same way. They enjoy the investigations sometimes, especially when it's a real mystery, even though murder is a terrible business. It's just the way it is. But we have to be careful, and never forget there's a maniac around somewhere, and maybe hiding in plain sight."

"Like here?" she asked, smiling as we stopped outside the family motorhome that had all the extras and must have cost a fortune.

"I think we can rule them out. I bet they didn't get a wink of sleep last night with the kids being excited. Although it's a strange way to spend Christmas for a family. Let's get this over with." With a sigh, I rapped on the door to the large motorhome, a pang of jealously surfacing as I imagined the space they had, and that they would most likely have at least two if not three bedrooms inside. Two, I decided, with a sofa turning into a bed for one of the children. I bet they had a big fridge, too, something I wished I had. As an ex-chef once at the top of his game, having to use a tiny under-counter one running off gas was probably the hardest thing I'd had to adjust to in my new life.

We scooped away as much snow as we could from the door while we waited, but because of the size of the vehicle the drifts weren't acting like a prison, but half the door was still covered.

As we worked, the door was opened then stuck fast against the snow. The cries of excited children from inside, and the father telling them to calm down, were loud but muffled as someone shoved at the door.

"The snow's blocking it," I said as the man's head peered out from the crack.

"Wow! Didn't realise it was that deep. The kids wanted to open presents before they came out to play, but how cool is this?" He smiled at us, clearly confused by our appearance, then turned back into the camper and shouted, "Kids, we have an issue. Hand me something to help shift the snow from the door. Something flat. Maybe the chopping boards."

The decibels rose as the children squealed and shouted for their mother, then the man returned and handed us two bright plastic chopping boards and asked, "Do you think you can clear it enough so I can get out, then I can help? And thanks for coming to warn us. We'd have been trapped otherwise."

"You'd have managed. We did, and we're in the VW," said Min with a smile.

"Cool van. You live in it?"

"I do. Min visits. I'm Max, by the way."

"Nice to meet you both. Um, let's say hello properly in a mo. And merry Christmas. I'm Sam. You can meet my family in a few. So, what can I do?"

"We'll get the door uncovered, then it'll be down to you. We have some news, and it's best if you come out alone. Sorry, that's cryptic. We'll explain, I promise." I got to work with the plastic chopping board, which was great for scooping the snow, and Min joined me. We cleared the drift in less than a minute, building up a welcome sweat.

We gave the all clear to Sam, so he opened the door then stepped out, closing it behind him. He wore a smart pair of Burberry Wellies, rather old-fashioned brown cords, a festive jumper with reindeer pulling Santa and his sleigh, and had slipped on a red and white bobble hat, hiding his short back and sides but leaving a thick mop of brown curls with a few grey hairs hanging over his forehead. He had a round belly, but just the usual middle-age spread and a slight dad bod. His open, friendly face, free of lines, and very good teeth screamed a generous income bracket, confirmed by an expensive watch poking through his sleeve as he held a hand out to shake.

"Thanks for that," he said, stepping down into the snow. "Wow, it must have come down like crazy in the night. Look at the drifts. Your van is almost buried. And the others too. Crazy. Awesome, though. It really feels like Christmas."

"It sure does," agreed Min. "Are you here for long?"

"A few days. It's unconventional coming away like this, but we love our motorhome and are always off somewhere or other. Usually, it's just in the summer, but this year I couldn't stand it."

"Stand what?" I asked.

Sam checked for eavesdroppers, then leaned in and said, "Family. I know, it's awful of me," he held his hands out, grinning as he admitted his guilt, "but I couldn't cope with another family get-together. It always turns sour, and the wife's folks are a right pain. This year I wanted it to be just us, so here we are, and boy am I glad we came. Snow, peace, and no arguments. Perfect. Just me, Jo, the two teens, and our little one."

Min and I exchanged a glance, then I told Sam, "I'm afraid it's not as idyllic as you think. Come with us, please."

"Um, sure, but what's this about? Is everything okay?"

"Not really, Sam. Let us show you."

We led the way to the snowman. Sam gasped, and whooped, "Awesome! Did you guys make it?"

"No, and we don't know who did. But look closer, Sam." I led him around to the front and we stopped before the terrible sight. Sam's eyes bugged as he realised what the issue was. He looked from me to Min, then back to the head of the poor man trapped inside. "I don't understand. He's dead? Inside a snowman? How? And why?"

"It's a real mystery. We found him not long ago. Our dog toppled the snowman's head and this is what we found. Do you recognise him?" I watched his reaction, which was one of shock and the right amount of fear and concern as he shook his head, lost for words.

"It's okay," soothed Min. "Seeing a dead body is hard to handle, but we had to show you. You need to keep everyone away, so maybe it's best to entertain the children inside until this has been cleared up."

"Yes, of course," he stammered. "This is terrible. Who would do such a thing?"

"We don't know."

"Poor guy. And on Christmas too. This is nuts. Have you called the police?"

"Yes, but with the weather they might be a while. If you do come out with the children, please stay away from any footprints and give it a wide berth. It's a crime scene, although with the fresh snow coming down, it's a lost cause." Min rubbed at Sam's shoulder as he stood, eyes glued to the snowman, arms limp at his sides.

"Of course. I'll keep everyone inside. How disturbing. Wish I'd put up with the in-laws now," he laughed, noting

Min's hand, then smiling weakly at her. "Is there anything I can do to help?"

"Not really," I said. "We'll tell the others staying here, then we'll go up to the house. Try to enjoy your Christmas, but be warned there will be police asking questions and utter chaos later on. This snow will make it difficult for the teams, and I'm not sure who will come, but it won't be very relaxing for quite a while once they arrive. I'd make the most of it until then. How old are the children?"

"The boys are thirteen. Twins. Still excited about Christmas and presents but trying to act grown up and failing miserably. The little one is two. We have a handful, for sure, but I wouldn't have it any other way."

"And none of you saw or heard anything last night or early this morning?" asked Min.

"Nothing. We got here, set up, then didn't come back outside. We decorated the motorhome then watched a movie. Once the little one was asleep, we played some games. I still can't believe this is real. He looks fake, like a mannequin's head or something. Who would do this?" Without waiting for an answer, he made his way back to the motorhome then went inside, clearly not acting himself as it was obvious he was usually a very upbeat, chatty guy.

Deciding we'd best get this over with, we made our way over to the old van the couple had arrived in last night. The TV blared as we approached, so I couldn't imagine how loud it was inside. Because of their position under the trees, they'd fared better than the other vehicles and although the drifts were high on one corner, most of their vehicle was visible and they could open the door at least.

"Think they'll hear if we knock?" I asked Min.

"If we bang loud enough. I hate this. It's like telling people they've lost a loved one. Breaking news of a murder is awful, even if people don't know who the deceased is."

"I know, but what choice do we have?"

"Drive off and stay somewhere else?"

"Should we?"

"Of course not! I was joking."

"So was I. Kind of." I winked at Min, but it would have been the simplest solution. Leave, enjoy our day, and let the authorities deal with it.

"What's all this racket?" asked a stout woman in her sixties, arms folded across her Christmas jumper of a smiling Santa with his red nose flashing.

"Oh, sorry, we were just about to knock," I shouted above the din of the TV.

"What? Speak up, boy. Why are you whispering?"

"I wasn't."

"What?"

"I said I wasn't whispering?" I hollered.

"Then why didn't you say so? Merry Christmas." The woman turned, then bellowed, "Turn that TV down. We have guests." She spun back to us, smiled, and grabbed my arm and said, "Come in. Come in. You're letting the heat out."

Before I could protest, she yanked me forward with surprising strength, and I had to take the two steps hastily or I'd have been flat on my face.

Chapter 5

Careening forward, I face-planted into a bank of cupboards opposite, then Min smashed into my back with a sharp exhale and the door slammed shut.

I began to sweat instantly, the heat stifling, the humidity dangerously high. Everyone knew damp was the enemy of vanlife, and once it started you best beware; mould would fester and proliferate, then it was game over. This couple clearly weren't concerned, and as I turned, I gasped, my OCD in overdrive as I was confronted with my idea of hell on wheels.

There was stuff absolutely everywhere in the ancient motorhome. Old-fashioned cupboards that'd seen better days had doors and drawers hanging off, stuffed beyond breaking point with clothes and general household items. Ornaments adorned every surface, held in place by railings around the counters and no doubt stuck in place or they'd be smashed.

The small kitchen area that bisected half of the vehicle was chock full of food in various states of preparation along with all manner of Christmas fare including a cake, crackers and biscuits, dishes of crisps, and a huge turkey surrounded by a tray of potatoes, both still raw, but prepped ready to go. The living room comprised two bench seats, a table, and a large TV on the wall opposite. A man was sprawled out on one seat, staring intently at the screen, the remote in his hand, already jabbing at the volume button. The bar sprang into life on the screen, climbing rapidly to max, and soon my eardrums were ready to burst as we were regaled with Christmas carols.

"Turn it off! We have guests," the woman snapped, marching over and snatching the remote from the man's hand then muting the TV. She turned back to us with a tut. "Sorry about him. He's as deaf as a post and twice as thick."

"I'm not the one who's deaf," he huffed, then smiled at us and clambered out from behind the table that caught his belly wrapped in a red shirt, his white beard and rosy complexion making me think of Santa and how he could easily pass for the big guy.

"Yes, you are! You have the TV too loud. Say hello to our guests."

"Who are they?"

"Why don't you ask them?" she grumbled, shaking her head then moving to the corner and peeling a potato, ignoring us completely.

"Who are you?"

"I'm Max. This is Min. We're in the VW."

"Ah, the classic campervan. Very nice. I'm David, this is Gina. We're old hands at this lark. Been taking our old girl out for thirty years now. We had her from new. You live in yours?"

"I do. Min visits."

"Not married, eh?" he asked with a frown, showing his old-fashioned values.

"It's complicated. We were, but I messed up, so we divorced, but we're seeing how things go and hopefully by —"

"Was I acting like I cared?" he asked, looking puzzled.

"You did ask."

"Just pulling your leg, son!" he guffawed, holding his belly as he bent almost double.

"My David thinks he's funny. He's the only one," shouted Gina, wielding her purple potato peeler.

"Sorry about that. Sounds like you two know what you're doing. We aren't vanlifers, but we do spend more time in this old wreck than at home. Especially out of season. The sites are cheaper, and it beats sitting inside staring at the TV."

"It can get costly," agreed Min.

I glanced over to the huge TV, unable to help myself, and David laughed. "Ah, yes, well, you know what I mean. And we do get out a lot, but it's the holidays and I wanted to relax. Enjoy the smells as Gina cooks dinner. Can't wait." David rubbed his hands together, clearly a fan of Christmas, and definitely of food.

"Stop hogging our guests," chastised Gina as she wiped her hands on an apron, loaded the turkey into the oven, then slammed the door shut with a satisfied grunt. She was about the same size as her husband, with matching white hair, red face, and a friendly demeanour. With an apron over her flashing jumper, a red skirt, and thick, green tights, she was as festive as David, and clearly enjoyed her food just as much.

"I wasn't. You were busy. When's dinner?" David licked his lips, waiting expectantly.

"About three hours. Maybe four."

"What!" David's shoulders slumped as he glanced at the oven and frowned, squinting to read the timer. "You sure? That can't be right, can it?"

"Love, it's nine in the morning. You only just had your breakfast. Lunch will be served at about two."

"But you just said it will be four hours. That's five."

"The turkey has to rest." Gina turned her back to her husband and from nowhere thrust a tray out and asked, "Mince pie? I made them myself."

"Gina makes a wicked mince pie. And the Christmas cake has been fermenting for two years now. She always does them well in advance. You'll have to come over and try some."

"It's not fermenting, you old fool," tutted Gina with a loving smile for him. "It's maturing. I always ensure we have a Christmas pudding that's at least two years old. Gives the best flavour."

"It really does. I wish I'd planned ahead like that. I had to buy one from Marks and Sparks."

"Nothing wrong with Marks and Spencer grub," said Gina. "They're great."

We both took an offered mince pie and congratulated her as they were exceptional. She was clearly an excellent cook and took it seriously, as she'd already prepped most of the food for their dinner and cooked David his breakfast, and I got the impression she wasn't one to sit around watching the TV like him.

"So, what do we owe the visit to?" asked David, nabbing another mince pie and getting a slapped hand from Gina.

"Yes, dears, why are you here? It's lovely to have visitors, of course, but haven't you got things to do? Were you just looking out for us and helping with the snow? That was very kind of you."

"It's rather an awkward situation," explained Min, glancing at me.

"Really? Do tell?" David was all ears, the TV forgotten, and he seemed to be hearing us fine now.

"There's been a murder," I declared, figuring it was best to get this over with.

"We have ourselves a pair of pranksters," laughed David, nudging Gina.

"Very funny," she said with a confused frown. "But I don't get the joke. What's the punchline?" Distracted, Gina picked up her peeler and began working on a pile of carrots there was no way it was possible for two people to eat, especially with everything else they'd be consuming.

"Sorry, maybe we should begin again. We were snowed in, but once we managed to get out we found a snowman. Our dog knocked the head off, and we discovered the head of a real person buried inside. We just told the family, and a guy called Kev in the Transit, so wanted to warn you too. There will be police all over the place soon, if they can get through the drifts, and we're about to head up to the house and warn the owners."

Gina and David were understandably sceptical and merely stared at us, open-mouthed, clearly still waiting for a punchline that would never come.

Carrot poised, then used to scratch an itch in a place that made me certain I'd refuse an invite for dinner if it was offered, Gina asked, "You're being serious?" then eyed the carrot with a frown before dumping it in her bowl of peelings.

"Don't be daft, love. They're messing around." David turned to us and asked, "Right?"

"Sorry, but no. Max is serious. It's all true. It's best if you stay away from the crime scene so the police can check it out, although it's quite messed up what with us and Anxious and your neighbour already taking a look."

"This I have got to see." David grinned, eyes dancing with excitement as he dragged a woolly hat over his head, pulled it down low, then asked, "Where are my gloves? And my coat? And my scarf? Come on, Gina, hurry up. We have a real mystery on our hands."

"Weren't you out there last night, love?" asked Gina. "Didn't you see anything?"

Min and I exchanged a look but said nothing. This was exactly why it always paid to talk to people in the area as soon as possible after a murder was committed. You simply never knew who it might be, and now we had a suspect. Especially as David's reaction was so strange.

"What? Eh? I didn't go outside!" David pulled his hat down even lower until his eyes were almost covered, then hurriedly wrapped the scarf Gina gave him around his neck, hiding the red flush creeping up to his cheeks.

"Yes, you did. Remember, we had that bottle of wine and you were desperate for a pee but didn't want to use our little portable one. I hate it too," she explained. "We don't like going to the toilet in our home. It feels wrong."

"I assumed you had a proper bathroom in here," said Min.

"Oh yes, we do, love, but we don't use it unless we really have to. All those nasty chemicals are terrible for the environment."

"It's a gross habit," grunted David, doing up the toggles on his red coat then standing there awkwardly, looking like Paddington Bear. If he had a Marmalade sandwich, he could have starred in the next movie.

"So you went outside?" I prompted. "Did you notice anything out of the ordinary?"

"I don't even remember," he snapped. "Maybe I did go out, but if I did it was before the snow. Didn't see a thing."

"What are you talking about?" Gina frowned at him then said, "You were covered in it. You said it was coming down really fast. I looked through the window and saw it. You don't remember?"

"Nope."

Gina's eyes welled and she looked away from David then moved closer to us and whispered, "His memory isn't what it used to be. He's not too bad most days, but sometimes he forgets things."

"Has he seen anyone? Had any tests?" asked Min.

"Oh, it's nothing like that. He isn't senile or anything, just a little forgetful sometimes. It happens to us all." Gina laughed, but it was forced, and she glanced over as David fumbled with the toggles then nodded before going to help him.

We nodded in sympathy, but I got the feeling Gina was making excuses, and that David remembered going out. But then something struck me and I asked, "Haven't you been outside this morning to use the facilities? And come to think of it, Sam hadn't been out either, which is strange. He has a wife and children in their van, which is a tight squeeze. They can't have all used a toilet inside."

"We always use our chemical one in the mornings for a pee and a poo," declared Gina merrily, slipping on a matching red duffle coat, her nimble fingers making short work of the toggles.

"But you said you didn't like to use it," said Min, shaking her head.

"Apart from in the morning. Are we ready?"

"You don't need to come," I told them. "It will mess up the crime scene and it's freezing out there."

"Nonsense. We might recognise him." David slipped on a pair of wellies Gina handed him from a cupboard, then pulled her own on and they stood there, faces expectant, so with a shrug Min and I stepped outside into the freezing cold and pulled our coats tight as we did them up.

We led the way, with the couple chatting excitedly behind us, commenting on how deep the snow was and yet upbeat and even throwing a few snowballs, enjoying the wild weather.

"Isn't it beautiful?" gasped Gina. "It never snows at Christmas. I always love it when it's like this. It's as though the world has been scrubbed clean and you can start again. Like it's perfect. Does that make sense?"

"Absolutely. Wait! Who's that?" Min grabbed my arm and yanked me back, then dragged me towards the others before whispering, "Everyone hide." Min performed a strange leap then landed flat on her chest, pulling me down with her. Gina and David followed, clearly keen to be involved in this intrigue, so we lay there, the fresh snow falling fast and covering us almost immediately, helping to hide the bright red coats.

"What's happening?" asked David.

"Over there." Min pointed, and we shielded our eyes to watch as a figure darted past the awning at the family motorhome, her head low against the snow, but wrapped in a Parka with a fur-lined hood, the classic green coat zipped right up so her face was hidden. I knew it was a woman, though, as her frame and gait made it obvious, and I could only assume it was Sam's wife, Jo, who we hadn't met yet.

"She's acting cagey," noted David. "What's she up to?"

"No idea. Let's watch and see." Min's eyes danced as she turned to me, caught up in the intrigue and enjoying herself immensely.

"It's not meant to be fun," I reminded her.

"Don't tell me you aren't excited and intrigued. She might have done it."

"Without her family knowing? They'd have missed her in the night."

"Not if they were asleep. Maybe she drugged them so they wouldn't wake up."

"Min, you're getting carried away. Calm down. A mother isn't going to drug her children, and what about the toddler? He's two."

"True. But it doesn't mean she didn't do it. Watch. She might give herself away."

We remained motionless and tried to track Sam's wife as she headed straight for the snowman, but the flurry came down so fast and hard and the wind had picked up, so visibility had dropped and it was impossible to see what she was doing. As best I could make out, she'd walked up to the snowman, stood for a while, then walked around it before hurrying away back to the van then going inside.

Min and I helped Gina and David to stand, then we brushed each other down and waded towards the snowman. I asked everyone to stop before we made even more of a mess of the scene, realising too late that it was pointless and already the woman's footprints were covered in fresh snow.

"It's definitely a real head," noted David, stepping closer but not too close.

"How awful," gasped Gina, then buried her head in Min's chest.

"Let's get you both back. David, do you recognise him? Gina, I hate to ask, but what about you?"

"Never seen the guy before." David studied the face for a while, then struggled over to Min and Gina. Gently, he spun his wife so she looked into his eyes and asked, "What about you, love? Recognise him?"

Gina's eyes darted to the corpse, then she shuddered and focused on David. "I've never seen that man before. But what's that?" She pointed to just in front of the snowman where something blue glinted before it was buried under the increasingly hostile snow falling so thick and fast I worried we'd be stranded out here if we stayed still for much longer.

"I'll go and check, but that couldn't have been here earlier or we'd have seen it."

"I did good, right?"

"You really did, Gina. Well done!"

Gina's chest swelled, but she couldn't look at the awful sight any longer and clung to David as he stroked her arm and spoke to her quietly.

Cautiously, and just about able to see the woman's footprints, I approached the object. I knew there was zero point worrying about preserving anything, so bent and retrieved what turned out to be an A5 spiral-bound notebook with a hard blue cover.

I held it up and the others smiled as I tucked it under my coat then retraced my steps.

"What is it?" asked Gina.

"A clue?" asked David.

"I think so, yes. Let's get inside and take a look. Want to come to the VW?"

"Let's get back to ours. There's more room," said David.

"Sure. Um, I'm not sure I should open it though. It's a book."

"Course you should. We need to know what we're up against." David nodded, face determined, so I decided maybe it was best we all took a look, although I had serious doubts about him and wondered if he'd seen the body last night and chose to ignore it, or was involved in a more sinister way. Whatever the truth, checking the book might help me figure him out and at least watch for a reaction.

A few minutes later, we were ensconced in the warmth of their motorhome and the book sat on the table with us standing around, unsure what to do next.

Chapter 6

"Open it then," encouraged David as he yanked off his hat, unwound his scarf, and shrugged out of his coat, face red, sweat on his brow.

Gina stripped back to her jumper and apron, just as red, and I knew we were the same as it truly was stifling inside. It couldn't be healthy, but it was more than welcome, and I was relieved to discover my nose was still intact after I gave it a squeeze.

"I'm not sure I should." I eyed the book warily, my curiosity building but knowing this was evidence and there might be fingerprints. Would the cold and snow have eradicated them? Did Sam's wife put the book there? If so, why?

"You definitely should," said Gina, nudging me in the ribs with surprising force.

"Min, what do you think?"

"We should look. It must be important. That woman dropped it."

"Did anyone actually see her do that?"

Nobody did, but it was a crazy coincidence otherwise, so, against my better judgement, but with curiosity getting the better of me, I kept my gloves on and brushed the melting snow from the cover. It was blank, but well-worn, and stained with oil. At least it wasn't blood, so we were off to a good start.

Flipping over to the first page, we were slightly disappointed to find random scribblings and rough line drawings of what to me looked like a diagram of a wall plate and joists with several angles written then crossed out. The next few pages were of similar things. Sums for building supplies, costs for materials, random numbers and odd words that made no sense to me, but I'm sure did to the builder who must have owned the book. We spent a few minutes going through it page by page, then I closed the book and thought for a moment.

"Just a builder's notebook," David said finally, his disappointment evident.

"Seems like it. It's just random stuff you'd write when you're working out materials or costing a job. No telephone numbers, names, or addresses though. Shame."

"Oh well, at least we tried our best." Gina waved dismissively, then strode with purpose over to the counter and resumed her carrot-peeling marathon.

With a knowing nod to Min, I retrieved the book, stowed it inside my jacket, then said, "Time for us to go. We need to inform Maddie and Roy. Nice to meet you both, and sorry to put a downer on your Christmas. Enjoy your dinner, and if you think of anything, please let us know."

"Shouldn't we tell the police, not you?" asked David.

"I guess you should," I chortled, rubbing at my thick beard, aware I was acting like we were the ones leading the investigation.

"Stay safe," said David, pumping first my hand then Min's vigorously.

"You too."

"Bye." Min kissed David's cheek, then went over and hugged Gina.

Feeling awkward, I gave Gina a peck on the cheek, unsure what was correct with people I'd just met, but she seemed to like it and beamed at me before staring at yet another carrot. How many did these people eat? Maybe they kept rabbits in the back room?

Wrapped up and back outside, we decided to check on Anxious. He was pining at the door by the time I got it open, the strong wind having created yet another snowdrift. He leapt into my arms and whined as he licked my face frantically and his tail thumped against my coat.

"Did you miss us?" I laughed, trying not to think about the fact I was standing on my collapsed gazebo that would now have to be thrown out. The last thing I wanted was to add to landfill, though, so maybe I could repurpose it and the poles to make an awning?

"Of course he did. Come on, let's get this over with. Breaking the news to Maddie and Roy will be tough, but we need to do it now. We'll have to tell the people in that massive motorhome later. Weird they haven't come out yet."

"Even more weird is that the kids haven't come out to play." I nodded to where the shouts and laughs of the children could be heard even above the howling wind.

"Sam will have told them to stay inside."

"Maybe, but it still seems odd."

We used our footsteps to make the going easier, then had to trudge across the thick snow towards the house. Any sign of a vehicle or person was long gone, the world painted fresh in blinding white, nothing but tiny bird tracks on the pristine covering.

We managed to get across the main camping field without too much bother as we skirted the tree line where the snow wasn't very thick, but once closer to the gate the going was impossible as drifts had piled the snow up to our waist. With no other choice, and with the wind having thankfully abated, we walked into the middle of the field then one achingly slow step at a time managed to get onto the track leading to the house.

The going was easier thanks to the road, but not by much. As we approached, the hum of a machine increased in volume, and for a moment I thought the police had arrived, but when we rounded the bend and I caught the back end of a yellow digger going down the track, I assumed it was Roy clearing the lane for access.

Spirits lifting, as at least we wouldn't be marooned, we sped up and hurried towards the house and the static home where smoke rose from the flue sticking out of the roof and the house's wonky brick chimney. I guessed they wanted to keep the main building dry so had a lit a fire there, too, but were also keeping their accommodation toasty.

"I hope the fire's roaring. I'm absolutely freezing." Min cuddled in close as we made the final approach, both our teeth chattering. Anxious was like a solid block of ice no matter how much I tried to keep him covered in a blanket and rubbed his back, and he was trembling. Little dogs can suffer in the bad weather, and although usually unaffected, the freezing temperatures were clearly getting to him.

With a sigh of relief, I rapped on the door, and we waited eagerly for Maddie to open it. It came as quite a shock when it was Roy who answered.

"Hey, guys. Wow, you look frozen. Come on in. Get warmed up. Is Anxious okay?"

"Thanks for the invite," said Min eagerly, wasting no time following Roy inside, closely followed by me after I let Anxious down.

"We appreciate it." I closed the door and removed my wellies then slipped off my coat, scarf, gloves, and hat, beaming at Min who had done the same. Her rosy cheeks gave me cheer, and I felt suddenly festive as I noted the tree with fairy lights, tinsel hanging everywhere, and even presents under the tree.

"Looks lovely in here. You made a real effort," noted Min.

"We adore Christmas, and it's the first one here so we went all out. Maddie's out clearing the snow, so I'm making a start on dinner, but I've been warned I'm on peeling duty only as I'm not the best cook."

"Same here. I leave the cooking to Max," said Min.

"Wish I was a good cook. I never seem to get the hang of it. I'm great with beans on toast, but anything too complicated and I glaze over and can't seem to follow the recipe. I'm better with physical work. And before you ask, yes, I know it's not usual for the man to be in and the woman outside working a digger, but Maddie's ace with the old machine and enjoys using it. It makes her feel useful as most heavy lifting is down to me. And besides, it's freezing out there!" Roy grinned as he winked, then beckoned us into the living room area where he bent and added a few small logs to the wood burner.

We gathered around eagerly, and as I thawed out I was a taken back to being a child. As the burning in my toes increased, I recalled coming in from playing in the snow, my wellies full of the stuff, my feet totally numb, then Mum pulling them off as I screamed in pain before sitting with my socks off, my bare feet bright red, the gas fire up to max, my toes hurting so bad as they thawed out.

Once I was warm, it would be straight back outside to repeat the whole process multiple times for as long as the amazing snow remained on the ground. The days stretched out like they would last forever, but all too soon darkness would descend and I'd spend the rest of the evening wrapped in my PJs and a dressing gown, watching awful shows on the TV with Mum and Dad and drinking hot chocolate. Perfect, and I wished I could go back to such days where my only concerns were whether I had enough socks and if dinner would be ready as soon as I'd finished playing with my friends.

"Max?" Min frowned, a smile on her face, clearly wondering where I'd drifted off to.

"Sorry, I was just remembering when I was a kid and my feet would burn like crazy when I sat in front of the gas fire to thaw out."

"I did that too!" squealed Min. "The full four bars!"

"And me. Those were the days, eh? No stress, no worries, just playing then in for dinner and sleeping like a log for ten hours. Perfect." Roy beckoned us to sit, then flopped down in front of the fire. Anxious graciously lay across his legs, as close to the fire as he dared. "Feeling the cold, eh, buddy?" Roy stroked his back and Anxious spread out, grinning.

We joined them on the floor and I felt better immediately, but after a quick glance at Min and her nodding to say I should tell Roy, I told the whole sorry tale.

"So he's really dead?"

"He sure is. I know this sounds like a joke, but trust me, it isn't. We don't know who he is or how he got there, but he's definitely there. Any ideas who he might be?" We described what he looked like but Roy came up blank, then I remembered the notebook so explained about the other guests and how it seemed like Sam's wife had left the book there, and about meeting David and Gina, then even about the presents in our van.

"Guess you were both good this year," chuckled Roy. "And before you ask, no, it wasn't us that left the gifts. It's a nice surprise, though, right?"

"Not really, as it means someone got into the van without us knowing. How did they do that? And why leave the presents?"

"It must have been Santa." Roy was serious, and we waited for a laugh that never came.

"Oh, um, yeah, it must have been," stammered Min, casting a surprised glance at me.

"Definitely. He hasn't visited me for years, but maybe it's because I'm new to vanlife that he thought a few presents would be nice."

"I bet that's it." Roy nodded knowingly, seemingly convinced Santa had taken the time to drop in on us last night.

"Roy," I began, hesitant about what I should tell him as the fact was we didn't know either him or his wife well and for all we knew one of them was the killer, "I have a few things to tell you about me."

"That sounds ominous." Roy's eyes roamed, as if he was uncomfortable about something other than the killing, then he focused on me and admitted, "Sorry, but this has me spooked. Mind if we go and get Maddie? I don't like the thought of her out there alone with a murderer on the loose."

"Of course. Sorry, we should have stayed outside and gone to warn her straight away."

"Don't be daft! It's not your fault. Let's get her now."

"Sure, and I can fill you both in later."

Roy explained that they'd both worked to shovel the snow from around the house and static home then out to the lane using snow shovels, and then Maddie had begun on the lane, although neither of them believed she'd be able to clear it right down to the main road. It would help, though, and meant everyone could drive at least partway to the village if supplies were needed.

Turns out, Maddie was a whizz with the digger and had used a large bucket attachment to scrape the snow off the track and dump it to the side, clearing the way in no time.

We stood watching for a while as she handled the machine with ease and expertise, belying the fact such things were difficult to learn and only a seasoned pro could make it look so easy. When she spotted us, she parked and jumped out, rubbing her hands together as she joined us, wrapped up in so many layers and with a bobble hat over her head and a snood hiding most of her face.

"Hey, guys. Sorry we haven't had the chance to clear the snow from the campsite yet. We figured everyone would be pleased to see it and maybe have a play, especially the kids, but I can clear a track if you want?"

"I think you'll have to hold off on that for a while," I said.

Roy nodded in agreement, then shifted over to Maddie so they faced us, and told her, "Max and Min have some terrible news, I'm afraid."

"What's wrong? Has something happened? Have your water pipes frozen?"

"We haven't actually checked yet," said Min, glancing at me.

"They should be okay. I insulated them, and it's only a single pipe from outside into the fresh water tank for the sink anyway. No biggie if it is frozen. Maddie, we just told Roy the news, but you need to know too." I took a deep breath, then explained what had happened this morning, telling her everything.

"That's terrible! Who would have done such a thing? Why? It makes no sense to treat someone like that. And the time it must have taken. What's the point?"

"That's what Max is going to find out. If you want?" asked Min.

Both frowned, not understanding, then Maddie said, "That's very kind, but won't the police solve it? Max, no offence, but why would you be able to figure this out?"

"This is what I wanted to talk to you both about. In a past life, I used to be a chef. I worked for several Michelin three-star restaurants and was at the very top of my game. It seems that my eye for detail and noting the small, often seemingly inconsequential things, has been the perfect way to learn how to solve murders. Since I began vanlife, I've been involved in a few mysteries and have managed to solve them and uncover the killer."

"You're that guy!" Maddie laughed, then gripped a glove between her teeth and pulled it off. She checked her pockets until she found her phone, then spent a moment bringing up a website. "Here's his wiki page. Max Effort, the amateur detective who keeps showing up the police and solving the crimes before they do. It's a whole page about you." She showed Roy, who whistled, impressed by the now rather extensive entries.

"Don't believe all that. My dad keeps it updated, and he's rather biased.

"I heard about you too. It's all over the internet. You're famous."

"I wouldn't say that, and it's becoming a problem with people recognising me now, but I do think we can help.

There's no guarantee we can solve this, but if you don't mind us looking into things we'll give it our best shot."

"I don't think that's a very good idea," said Roy.

"Why not?" asked Maddie. "If they want to help, we should let them. Roy, we have a murderer around here. At our home. This is our livelihood. We can't let all our work be for nothing. The effort we've made, the money invested. It's our future. What if someone's trying to scare us off? What if the killer strikes again?"

"That's exactly why we should leave this well alone and let the police handle it. Look, guys, I appreciate the offer, and I know you're being kind, but what if something happened to you? I'd never be able to live with myself if you were next. Just try to enjoy your Christmas, and I'm so sorry you had to see the poor man like that, but please don't get involved."

"Maybe Roy's right. Maybe you should leave it to the professionals." Maddie smiled weakly at Roy and squeezed his hand before hastily stowing her phone and putting her glove back on. "Gosh, it's so cold. I suppose I better see if I can get the entire track cleared so the police can make it up here. Assuming the main road has been done, which is very unlikely. Every little helps, right?"

"Of course," I agreed. "But listen, both of you. We honestly don't mind looking into this if we think of anything that might help. I'm not even saying we'll be of any use, but this is our call and we want to have your permission if something crops up. How does that sound?"

Our hosts exchanged a look, then Roy nodded and Maddie whooped as he said, "That would be fine. Thank you. But be careful, and please try to enjoy your day. Don't put yourself in danger, and have fun. Easier said than done now, I suppose, but it is Christmas."

"That's right. If you need anything, let us know. I better not clear the campsite of snow in case the police want everything left as it is."

"Yes, wait until they arrive and see what they say," I agreed. "We're so sorry this happened, as this is your business, but just one more question."

"Sure," said Roy.

"Do you recognise this book or the man in the snowman?" I showed them a photo of the man, then the book, but neither had seen him before or the book and all the work so far had been done by them, not a builder, so why it was here was a mystery. We thanked them, and went to leave, but they insisted on coming with us so they could see the body for themselves.

Chapter 7

As we retraced our steps and trudged through the increasingly thick snow, I took some time to actually enjoy the beautiful day. The wind had completely died down, enveloping us in a world of absolute silence apart from the crunch of our boots.

I immersed myself in that strange quietude only snow afforded, enthralled by the white winter wonderland that had utterly transformed the world, turning everything into a sparkling, pristine arena to play in, or, in our case, walk towards a corpse.

For a few beautiful minutes all that was forgotten, and I let my senses reach out, listening to the birds begin to stir after hunkering down for the storm, the drips of melting ice falling from the branches weighed down with the snow, even the occasional snap of a twig as the weight became too much.

How wonderful it was, yet so different to the green our country was known for, and it took me aback as I glanced left then right, not a single blade of grass evident. Living in a place where snow was around for months on end must be a strange thing, as although it was special and serene, I couldn't imagine a world without green.

The others were silent, caught up in the peculiar atmosphere, the tension palpable the closer we got, and once we arrived and stood before the gruesome snowman, the spell was broken as Maddie gasped and Roy rubbed his eyes as he hissed through his teeth in shock.

"What a terrible thing to do," sighed Roy. "Why would anyone go to such trouble?"

"It's a weird one, that's for sure," I replied.

"I wonder how he was killed," mused Maddie. "Should we take a look? It seems wrong to leave him like that. It's disrespectful. The poor man deserves better. But who is he? How did he get here? There were no signs of a vehicle on the lane, although I suppose the snow will have hidden any tyre tracks."

"There wasn't even a faint trace?" I asked, turning to her.

"No, nothing. Mind you, I was up in the digger, so maybe if I'd checked there would have been some sign. Doubtful, though, as it came down so heavy."

"And we didn't hear a disturbance last night. It was really quiet outside. The motion sensors didn't come on, and we heard nothing. We watched TV until about eleven, and had a few drinks, but this must have been done much later, surely?"

"I'm assuming it was in the middle of the night, but it's a guess. Gina reckons David went out for a pee quite late but he can't remember. He wasn't happy about Gina telling us, but I can't see him missing something like this."

"He is rather forgetful," said Min. "Maybe he was half asleep and didn't even notice. Gina said it had begun to snow by then."

"What about the other guests?" asked Roy. "Have you spoken to everyone?"

"We met Sam, but not his wife. But like I said, we saw her, at least assume it was her, walk from by their van then over to the snowman, then we found the notebook. We haven't met the children or her properly though."

"They seem very nice, and just wanted a quiet break as a family for Christmas. Now it's ruined. This is an awful start to our business." Maddie took a moment to study the vehicles, no signs of life beyond noise from the family pitch, but we didn't see anyone.

"What about the other couple who arrived late last night? What time was that, Roy?"

"About ten. They were oddballs, but very friendly. They liked to hug. Very keen to get here, but apparently they got lost on the way and were meant to be here hours earlier. It was no biggie, though, and they didn't seem the type to commit murders."

"Trust me, and I speak from experience, the killer is usually the last person you suspect. We'll go and have a chat with them in a while. If that's okay, of course?"

"Sure. Shall we leave it to you to tell them, or should we do that?"

"We'll do it. Maybe we'll get some information from them. We'll let you know if we do."

"Great! Well, I know this is awful, but we better get back to work. We have the track to clear and dinner to make, and we need to salvage what we can from this terrible morning and try to enjoy Christmas." Roy linked arms with Maddie and with a sorrowful smile they left.

Anxious, who had been uncharacteristically quiet, not even mithering for a fuss, stirred in my arms then whimpered quietly, eyes following the retreating couple.

"He's trying to tell us something," noted Min with a curious frown. "Max, was it just me, or was that whole situation odd. I don't mean really weird, but I definitely got a strange vibe. Shouldn't they have been more freaked out? I mean, like, totally freaked out. There's a dead dude in a snowman on their property and they had a quick look then went back to making dinner and clearing the track. Is it just me? Am I overthinking this?"

"No. You're right. The more murders I get involved in, the more astonished I am by people's reactions. Some take it well, others freak out. But when it happens at people's homes, they're always the most concerned. Those two handled it really well, maybe too well. They're new campsite owners putting all their savings and efforts into setting up the business, but didn't get very upset about the corpse."

"Maybe they're just not easily stressed. It was odd though. You'd think they'd have asked more questions about you calling the police and how the other people here reacted. Maybe want to go and talk to them. They haven't seen anyone else. Surely that's part of their job?"

"Like you said, they're new to this. But yes, if it was me, I'd be doing the rounds. Min, I don't think we should push this too hard. Maybe take a backseat on this one unless we uncover something obvious. It's Christmas and I want to enjoy it."

"Agreed. We should try to make the most of the day. Although, with a dead man right here, that will be tough."

"We'll get through it, because we're together." I bent at the knee and kissed Min's cold cheek. My reward a smile and a kiss in return.

Anxious whined again, eyes tracking after Maddie and Roy, which gave me cause for concern. Did he know something we didn't, or was he merely regretting not asking for cuddles?

"Think it might be them, or one of them?" I asked Min.

"I honestly don't know. There's no logic to it if they did it. This isn't good for business and word will definitely get out. Maybe it's something personal and that's why this man was turned into a snowman. What could the reason be?"

"I have absolutely no idea. Let's get inside and warm up. As much as I love the snow, I'm freezing."

"What about the other motorhome?"

We studied the large vehicle tucked under the trees, but there were no signs of life and with the snow now so thick I knew it would be a struggle to get there.

"You're right, we should go there now. I'm surprised it's down to us though."

"We did offer, and said we didn't mind."

"I know, but still. Shouldn't they have said no and done it themselves? I'm also concerned about Sam's wife. I can't imagine the woman we saw was anyone else, so what was she up to? Should we go and chat to her? And David's a worry too. I got the impression he remembered going out last night, but didn't want us to know. What's that about?"

"Let's get warm and have a think. And don't forget, there are presents under the tree," she teased with a smile.

"You're dying to open them, aren't you?"

"And you aren't?" she asked, shocked.

"I feel nervous, is what I feel. This has not been the fun, relaxing morning I'd envisioned. Come on, let's go home. Everything else can wait a while."

"Even the presents?"

"Apart from them. If we wait any longer, you're liable to explode. And we need to get dinner on the go or we won't be having a Christmas feast."

"One-pot wonder?"

"Maybe just this once we need to go all-out and use every pot and pan and to hell with the washing up!"

"No way! Max, what about your vow to use a single pot every day? Your cast-iron might go rusty."

Laughing, I said, "I think it can handle a day off. As for rust, you might be right. All the kitchen stuff is buried under the snow."

Arm in arm, with Anxious snoring in my other arm, we turned from the snowman and took a final check around the site before going home.

As we did, a cry made us turn back towards the entrance to our small hidden field to see a man brush himself down after recovering from a fall. He was covered in snow from head to toe, his steely buzzcut white with fresh fall and his trench coat the same. With a frown, he patted his chest then scooped snow from his pockets before pulling out a notebook and scribbling before stowing the items.

"Who's that?" Min pulled me closer and nudged me, like I hadn't seen him, clearly unsettled.

"No idea. From the motorhome, maybe? He looks exhausted. Ah, maybe it's the police? I'm amazed anyone made it. Let's go and ask."

But there was no need, as the moment the man spotted us he waded through the snow, cursing as he went, pointing at us as though we were to blame.

"Don't go anywhere," he barked once he was in earshot.

"Who are you?" called Min in return.

"DI Carroll. I'm the lead on this investigation. In fact," he huffed, stopping a few feet from us, "I doubt anyone else will make it. Took me ages to get here. Damn, but that hill was tough going. Had to walk the entire way. Shame the owners hadn't cleared it earlier. Bit pointless anyway, as everything's already covered in snow again. It'll be another day of this, if not more, which is just my luck."

The detective was mid-to-late forties, although I was never great at guessing ages, with a rather moribund expression. Heavy lids, bags under his eyes, with sallow skin tinged almost yellow meant he was a late-night drinker, confirmed by the hard round stomach protruding against his trench coat. His body was otherwise slim, a sure sign of a boozer for decades. The buzzcut was fresh, the stubble a few days old, his teeth rather stained. But despite the grim, serious demeanour, I took to him as beneath the dour exterior I could tell there was a fine human being who craved laughter but had been beaten down by life for whatever reason.

If I had to hazard a guess, I would say this was a hard-working detective who prided himself on his work ethic but had become recently divorced in the last few years and bad habits had increased once there was nobody to keep him in check. He'd most likely spent a lifetime working long shifts and had little clue about running a house and fending for himself properly.

"What are you gawping at?"

"Sorry, just sizing you up," I said honestly.

"You look like the kind of guy who is good at reading people, but let me spare you the trouble. Mid-forties, divorced three years, still hitting the booze hard as I'm so damn sad, and haven't got a clue how to cook properly or even what electricity company I'm paying a fortune to each month. I work hard, play hard, excuse the cliche, but my job means a lot to me. How did I do?"

"Pretty good," I laughed. "I was spot on. Now your turn."

With a frown of concentration, DI Carroll sized us both up, then said, "Divorced. From this lady, I assume. She divorced you, meaning it was your fault. You love each other, are trying to make a go of it, and most likely will get back together at some point unless you screw it up. I'd say you are, or were, a chef, and you," he pointed to Min, "look like you are a kind, caring person, and excuse me being so personal, but with such a trim figure, noticeable even through your layers, I'd say you either train people in gyms or... Ah, yes, a dietitian. And the van you were heading towards is for living in, so I'm guessing that you," this time I got the finger pointed at me, "live in it full-time. How'd I do?"

"Amazing!" we gushed.

"That's fine detective work to read that much on first impressions," I added,

"Or I checked you out on my phone on the way up after I was told your names. Max Effort, the scourge of the local detectives wherever he goes, with his beautiful ex-wife Min often making an appearance."

I chuckled. "Well done. We believed you for a moment."

"We really did. Hi, I'm Min, although I guess you already know that." Min extended a hand and they shook, then I did the same.

"Nice to meet you both. Look, I spoke to the owners and they explained the basics, but apparently you two found the body and have informed some of the people staying here. Care to tell me everything? No prizes for guessing where the stiff is. And boy must he be stiff by now." DI Carroll ignored Anxious who was desperate for a fuss, and turned his attention to the reason he was here.

"We found him earlier. We were excited by the snow, and then this little guy knocked the head off and released the body."

DI Carroll spun and asked, "Little guy?"

"Anxious. It's his name, not his emotional state." I nodded down to the squirming pooch and smiled.

DI Carroll took a step back in shock and laughed. "Hell, I didn't know that was real. It's a Jack Russell, right?"

"Um, yeah. What did you think he was if he wasn't real?"

"A Christmas present. A stuffed toy or something. A hand warmer? Hey there, buddy. I'm Clarence. No need to be formal and call me detective. Isn't he cute?" Clarence stroked Anxious and scratched behind his ears. His favourite, along with belly rubs, tickles, and general adoration.

"He's real, and it would be odd for me to be cuddling a stuffed toy dog, wouldn't it?"

"Not if you were given it by Min. Now, back to work. Please continue. What happened next?"

Min and I recounted the tale between us, leaving nothing out, and handing over the notebook which he inspected then bagged, not a word about it being the wrong thing to do.

When he'd finished asking questions, he stared at the corpse for the longest time, then told us, "I've seen enough for now. This damn snow has made it impossible to follow any tracks, and no team will be coming today. It's lucky I made it, but that's because I live down in the village and could walk. Nobody else is so local and the roads are impassable. Looks like it's up to us today, guys." Clarence smiled weakly, clearly uncomfortable with the situation, but at least he was friendly in his own rather dour way.

"You want our help?"

"What!? No, absolutely not! I was messing with you guys. Leave this to me. I know I look like an alcoholic deadbeat, but—" we protested, but he continued, "—I'm a great detective. This is my life, especially now, and I always get my killer."

"Always?" I asked, impressed.

"Don't be dumb! Sorry, that was rude. No cop ever always catches the criminal. I do better than anyone else though. I'm thorough, I never give up, and I'll stick with this until I'm done. Which means until I catch the murderer. So, to start, I'll talk to everyone here, and see what they have to say for themselves. From what you told me, there are a few issues already. People aren't being honest, and this notebook thing is intriguing. I'll take a proper look at it later. First, interviews."

"Will there really not be anyone else coming?" asked Min.

"It's doubtful. It's Christmas, the roads are a mess, and people have families."

"What about you?" Min smiled as she put a hand to his shoulder, straight into mothering mode. "Would you have been alone today?"

"Today and every day. The wife is gone, there are no children, my parents passed years ago, a terrible time, so it's just me now. I have a few friends, so I'm not a total loner, but I like my own space and the Jack keeps me company."

"Oh, so you do have a friend for today?" Min brightened and nodded to me with a warm smile.

"Min, he means the Jack Daniels."

"Oh, right. That's a shame."

"You can't beat Jack and coke," said Clarence wistfully, clearly craving a drink already.

"You can come to ours," I blurted, feeling sorry for him, but knowing I should have asked Min first.

"Thanks for the offer, but that's not very professional. And besides, I have a packed lunch."

"On Christmas Day? That's not right." Min nodded to me and told him, "You are invited. It's rude to say no. Please come."

"Thank you, but I won't. I'll have my hands full with the case, anyway. Max, I know you've solved plenty of murders, but take a day off. Relax, enjoy yourselves, and ignore me. Go about your day like normal. But before you do that, there is one tiny favour you can do me."

"Why do I get the feeling I'm not going to like this?" I sighed.

Clarence laughed loudly, startling Anxious from his doze, then said, "Because you're going to absolutely hate it!"

Chapter 8

Sighing, and with a longing glance at Vee where meal prep and cosy cuddles on the bench seat awaited, I asked, "You want me to help get the body out of the snowman, don't you?"

Slapping me on the back, he bellowed, "Nailed it!" then chuckled.

"Count me out," pouted Min. "I can't feel my fingers as it is."

"It shouldn't take long," I told her, praying we wouldn't uncover anything nasty. Or nastier than it already was.

"I'll get the kettle on and start peeling."

"Don't open the presents without me."

"I won't." Min winked, then took Anxious from me and cuddled him tight. He didn't even stir. The cold and excitement had got to him, and yet he was getting all the rewards. I longed for the same attention, but knew it would have to wait, and much longer than a few hours.

Watching her go, wistful, I focused on Clarence when he coughed to get my attention. "Sorry about this, and I know it's a special day, but I could do with the help."

"Sure. No problem. Thanks for coming. I bet it was a nightmare making it up here. Did it take long?"

"Hours. I got the call straight after you reported it, as my boss knew I was the most likely to actually follow through. The saddo who would be alone at Christmas. I don't see myself like that, although I guess I am that guy." Clarence shrugged; it was what it was.

"Our offer stands. You're welcome to join us."

"Max, that's so kind, but like I said, I'll pass. It's not professional, and who wants a functioning alcoholic divorcee copper for Christmas dinner? It's the worst possible combination. I'll get plastered and begin moaning about my life rather than enjoying the day."

"I don't think you'd do that at all. And besides, you're on duty."

"Yeah, well, tell that to this guy." Clarence pulled out a silver hip flask and took a long pull, then wiped his mouth with the back of his hand. "See? I'm a lost cause."

"I don't believe you usually drink on duty. You're playing up so I won't insist on you coming for dinner. I bet you won't have more than a few sips while you work the case. You're a dedicated detective. I can tell."

"Yeah, maybe," he grumbled, stowing the flask. "Let's get this poor guy out of there and give him some dignity."

We hunted along the tree line and managed to find some suitable dead branches, the snow thumping down around us as we disturbed the weighty bows, then returned to the snowman and carefully we began freeing the man.

Once we started, it was relatively quick, and the compacted snow forming the main body came away in large lumps, revealing the victim beneath. Our eyes widened in shock at what we discovered, but we said nothing, just continued until the ground was flattened and brown as we churned up the grass and soil beneath. Eventually, we managed to haul him free then lowered him gently before he toppled over.

Clarence and I stood back, removing our hats and wiping at our foreheads, the sweat from our hard work warming us both until we began to feel uncomfortable.

"Are you going to say it, or shall I?" I asked.

"You say it," he grunted, pulling out his flask, eyeing it dubiously, then returning it to his pocket without drinking.

"Somebody killed Father Christmas."

"Looks that way. Obviously, he's not the real one, but he sure looks the part. I wonder where his fake beard is, and his hat. Did you see anything like that around here?"

"No. Maybe it's in the remaining snowman. There's still quite a bit left lower down."

"Then let's check. We need to ensure we don't overlook anything before we decide what to do with him."

We got back to work, and I tried my best to ignore the strange corpse beside us as we methodically shifted the rest of the snowman and broke everything into small lumps so we could be certain we hadn't missed anything. We did indeed find a red hat with white fur trim and a pom-pom on top, and even the soggy fake beard, but there was nothing else.

With the man laid out and the hat and beard placed on his chest, we studied what we'd uncovered. It was not a pleasant sight. The man's flesh was blue bordering on black where it was exposed, his neck the worst besides his dark fingertips where the blood had pooled. He wore a very good quality Father Christmas outfit, not the cheap synthetic stuff you usually see, with a sturdy pair of thick rubber boots, shiny black and incongruous against the white snow.

"He's not got the build for Santa. He's too thin."

"I wouldn't call him skinny, but yes, no massive belly. His belt's even had a new notch made. Look." I squatted beside the man and Clarence joined me, and he lifted the long end with his stick.

"Either he's lost a lot of weight since he last wore it, or this is someone else's suit. See how the arms and legs have been rolled over a few times too? The suit's too large for him. He looks the part, mind you. It's very convincing."

"You don't think he's…" I trailed off, shaking my head and laughing at how carried away I was getting.

"The real Santa?" Clarence raised an eyebrow and smiled, but there was an uncertainty there, and he frowned as he studied the man again.

"Sorry, I was being silly. Of course it isn't. But it's odd that the suit was a little large. Maybe this was all they had at the place he bought it from."

"Probably. It's not like they come in many different sizes. I bet he just couldn't find anything better. More likely, it's someone who has lost the weight though. Let's check." Clarence scooted forward and fumbled with the belt then lifted the jacket to reveal a white vest beneath that fit snugly. He pulled it out of the trousers, revealing a trim waist but with loose skin beneath the belly button. The DI grunted, then tucked the vest in, buttoned the top, and fastened the belt again.

"Yep, guy's lost plenty of weight, and quite fast, leaving him with loose skin. I bet last year this fit him really well."

"I think you're right. So, we're looking for someone who killed a Santa impersonator. Which means?"

"Hey, don't ask me." Clarence threw his arms in the air then stood, shaking his head and muttering to himself as he walked around the corpse, studying every last detail. This was clearly a man who knew what he was doing and was already thinking several steps ahead and trying to get a picture of the most likely reason why any of this had happened. I bet he had a handful of theories already. It was impressive and interesting to watch, as usually I was pulled away from the crime scene before I got to study the detectives at work.

While Clarence made copious notes in-between taking photographs, I figured maybe I should take more photos, too, so snapped away, focusing on things I believed might be significant like the belt, hat, and beard. I figured it couldn't hurt, unless I got stopped by an eager cop and they asked me why I had pictures of a dead dude in the snow. That would take some explaining.

Once we'd both finished, we stood side by side and yet again studied the poor man.

"He looks almost peaceful," I noted. "Usually victims have a terrible expression as they knew it was coming, but this man seems like he didn't know a thing."

"He certainly doesn't look shocked. Now, there's one massive problem with this whole picture, and I'm sure you know what that is, right?"

"I do. We don't know how he died. For all we know, it might not even have been murder. Sure, someone did this to him and it's not very dignified, but we don't actually know he was killed on purpose."

"We do not. Meaning, we need to flip him over and check him out thoroughly to ensure there are no obvious signs of foul play. You ready?"

"As I'll ever be." With the cold creeping into my bones now our exertions had ceased, I slipped on my hat and gloves then bent beside Clarence and together we rolled the man over.

"Guess we can rule out accidental death," said Clarence in little more than a whisper, as though the snow that had begun to fall again demanded silence.

"There's little doubt about that. With a wound like that to the back, I can't see that anyone could survive. His ribs are showing." I stared in morbid fascination at the terrible wound that had ripped through the Santa outfit and his vest, tearing away flesh and revealing what ought to never be seen.

"Either he was dragged over rough ground until the suit split, or someone got busy with a massive cheese grater. See how the material is frayed at the edges and the skin is scratched around the exposed bone? I've seen this before in car crashes where the person's been catapulted from their vehicle then skidded along the road. Especially with motorbike accidents. It's never pretty." Clarence patted his pocket, as if reassured that his flask was still there, but he didn't drink.

"So it might have been a car accident?"

"Or motorbike. It would explain why the tracks covered over so easily."

"That doesn't explain what he's doing here, though, does it?"

"No, it doesn't. And with all the snow, there's no way he could sustain this kind of injury. The fact there's no blood here means he'd stopped bleeding before he was entombed, so at least we know he was dead before being made to look so ridiculous."

"But he was still dragged or carried here, then someone had to begin building the snowman, then prop him up inside it and continue packing snow around him. I know there were branches inside for support, but it would have been really difficult to do."

"Unless there was more than one person involved. That's the working hypothesis for this. Yes, a sole person could do it, but it would be immensely difficult. Much easier with two. One to hold him up, the other to build the snowman."

"Something doesn't ring true about any of this," I said. "Why go to so much trouble? Why hide him in plain sight like this?" They must have known he'd be discovered."

"Maybe they assumed it would be days, and not until the snow melted, before he was discovered. Or they wanted him found today. Plenty to think about." Clarence stood, his knees creaking. He cricked out his back by leaning and stretching, then sighed and said, "Now we need to move him somewhere out of the way. You up for that?"

"Sure. What did you have in mind?"

"Let's get him up to the house. There are a few outbuildings there so we can stow him out of the weather. I'm sure the owners will be accommodating."

"Whatever you think is best. It's a long way through this snow though. Mind waiting here for a few minutes? I have an idea."

"Sure. I want to go over a few more things anyway."

Leaving the DI to it, still in two minds about the man but warming to him as he seemed genuinely nice, but the drinking was an issue, I stomped through the snow, following my own footsteps to make the going at least a little easier, then continued past the house and down the lane until I caught up with Maddie.

She was more than happy to accommodate my request, and the best part was I got to hitch a ride in the cab of the digger back to the campsite. The digger tracks made short work of the trip, going over the snow without issue, and I wondered yet again why Maddie was so focused on the lane but had completely neglected the campsite, especially the route to the body. I got that it was best not to disturb a crime scene, but surely she should have begun clearing the site this morning before she even knew about the body?

Maddie was focused as she drove, and didn't say a word once she'd agreed, so I was pleased to get out when she pulled up.

"We'll load him into the bucket if that's okay, and are you sure we can store him in the barn?"

"Of course. The poor man. Should I stay here, or come out and help?"

"It might be worth taking another look at him now he's free of the snow. Maybe it will spark a memory. It's rather gruesome, so if you'd rather not, that's okay."

"I should see." Maddie was determined, and jumped out and landed beside me, wrapping her scarf around her neck a few times and pulling her hat low, then we approached the DI who was bent over the body, making notes.

"It's Santa," she gasped, staggering backwards and reaching for the digger bucket to steady herself. "Why would anyone kill him?"

I felt bad for not mentioning it, but wanted to judge her reaction, and there was no doubt she was shocked by the sight. At least Clarence had rolled the man over so Maddie didn't have to see the wound.

Clarence turned and focused on Maddie, as if he could read her inner thoughts, and it made me shiver. There was more to this guy than he was letting on. Much more. I couldn't put my finger on it, but it was almost as if he was playing a role, and this was him letting his act down. Somehow, he just seemed more professional, and was watching for any telltale giveaway signs that Maddie might make.

"You still don't recognise him?" he asked.

"Santa? Everyone knows what he looks like."

"The man you see before you isn't Father Christmas. I think we can all agree on that. He's wearing a suit too big for him, has recently lost a lot of weight, and is certainly not capable of delivering presents. Remember, in parts of the world it is still Christmas Eve, and children will be fast asleep, dreaming of him arriving."

"Gosh, yes, of course. I never thought about it like that."

"You didn't?" I asked, surprised. "I thought all kids asked their parents how could Santa possibly deliver all the gifts in just a few hours, and the reason is always the same. It's the time difference that makes it possible."

"I suppose you're right, but no, it never crossed my mind. As to the question," Maddie stepped closer and squatted to study the man properly, "I have never seen him before. Even if he looked different with more weight, I'm sure I'd recognise him." She stood and looked away, shaking her head to get rid of the image.

"Let's load him up and put him into storage. You okay with that, Miss?"

"Detective, I already told you, please call me Maddie. We appreciate all you're doing, and this is the least we can do. We aren't short of room, and I'm sure the guests would appreciate him being out of the way. Do you have any clues? Does he have ID? Any ideas at all?"

"Nothing on him bar a generic Casio watch, a single silver bracelet, and no phone or identification. He's a real mystery."

"Shame. What happens next?" Maddie glanced around the site with a worried frown, I assumed concerned the guests would come out to see what was happening and she'd have to deal with them.

"We move the body, then I ask everyone endless annoying questions." Clarence guffawed, rather out of character, then turned sombre as he added, "Why didn't you come and clear the campsite before the track? All other roads are impassible, so what's the point? Why not serve your guests first?"

"I honestly don't know. Roy said I should. He figured people might want to get out for the day, so I should do the track first to give it time to clear properly once the worst of the snow was removed, then he'd do the fields and tow people if need be."

"Where would people go on a day like today?" asked Clarence.

Maddie shrugged. "For a walk. To the pub or the local shop for emergency stuffing mix. They're open twenty-four-seven, every day of the year. The staff must hate it."

"The shop's open?" I asked, surprised but pleased as there were a few things I could do with getting and I did fancy a walk too. Anxious would enjoy the cleared track, and Min always adored walking in the snow.

"Yep. But I bet it's super quiet. Mind you, the pubs are probably busy. People won't let a little snow stop them from getting their Christmas pints in."

"Indeed." Clarence's eyes flashed with excitement, clearly wishing he was in the pub sipping on a pint by a roaring log fire rather than freezing in a field next to a corpse.

"Shall I lower the bucket?" Without waiting for an answer, Maddie rushed back to the digger and jumped into the cab.

I only just managed to jump aside before she lowered the bucket which slammed into the ground with enough force to have flattened me.

"Whoops!" she called out of the window, a cheesy grin on her face.

I wasn't amused, and neither was Clarence as we exchanged a look.

Chapter 9

With the body stowed safely in the barn, but no sign of Roy, we left Maddie to continue her seemingly pointless track clearing. Returning to the campsite, Clarence and I said our goodbyes for now, but he promised to check in later and insisted he'd be around for a good few hours interviewing people and generally getting a feel for the place.

To me, it was clear he preferred to be working than sitting at home alone, and I didn't blame him. The holidays were a trying time for many people. The stress of being around family for extended periods, and having to accommodate guests, let alone cook and clean for them and have people staying in your house who otherwise wouldn't meant stress levels rose dramatically. But this was as nothing compared to the loneliness millions of people in the UK suffered when the holidays came around.

I'd been shocked years ago when I saw a news report that gave the numbers of suicides at Christmas time, and that millions of people didn't see a single soul for the entire period. Not that the holidays were an exception to the rule. For many, the only other people they ever saw were when they went to the shops. The truth of the matter was that for a large part of the population they had no real friends. I was one of those people. Without Min, Anxious, and my folks, I would be alone. What would that be like?

I had no real experience of being truly alone. Work had always consumed me, and others were always around, and Min and I were always together until everything went wrong. Now I had Anxious, and vanlife seemed to have brought with it no end of new encounters. Some of the people I'd met were definitely classed as friends, but not the kind I got to hang out with regularly. To be totally alone, with no job, nothing to do, and nobody to talk to would be a very different life indeed, and I wondered how I'd cope with that.

My guess was not very well. I wished I could reach out to everyone and offer friendship or advice, but I couldn't. Instead, I sent positive energy out into the void, hoping it would improve things for anyone that needed it.

Distracted by my own thoughts, I found myself outside Vee without having consciously walked there. My heart beat faster, my spirits lifted, and I thanked my lucky stars that I had Min in my life, and the little guy, of course. I stopped and covered my mouth to stop my laugh escaping as I listened like a sneak to Min talking to Anxious, asking what he thought of her peeling skills, and his opinion on the tinsel she was re-arranging, happy beyond words to hear such everyday chatter and positive vibes emanating from the home I adored more than I often thought was sensible. But I didn't care. I loved my van, I loved Min and Anxious, and I loved my life.

"Hi, honey, I'm home," I sang out as I opened the door and stepped inside.

"Get your wellies off, you utter stinkpot," scolded Min, wagging a peeler at me.

Anxious sniggered from the bench seat, then returned to casting his expert gaze over the decorations.

"Bit harsh," I muttered, stifling a laugh. "And I was going to do it without you asking anyway." I sat and removed my wellies, aware that there was zero space to stow dirty boots, or much else for that matter. "Hey, where are yours?"

"In the back where they belong."

"So, what are you wearing?" My words trailed off as my eyes lowered to Min's feet, eliciting a gasp. By the time my eyes raised to meet hers, I was fit to bursting, and teased, "You're wearing Crocs! You said you'd rather be dead in a ditch than ever be seen in such crimes against fashion. Let me put mine on, and we can compare how awesome we look."

"Do not say another word about it. They're strictly van slippers. Yes, they are comfortable, and yes, they let my toes spread out nicely, and yes, it's like a foot massage, but no, I will never be seen wearing them outside."

"Not in this weather anyway. Although, does this mean you wore them after you stowed your wellies? You'd have got covered in snow."

"I put bags over my feet," she mumbled, then turned away, dangling tinsel like I didn't know her game.

"Ha! You love them! You were wrong, and I was right."

Min smiled and ordered, "Shut up!"

I slipped on my own Crocs, nice and clean and for inside the van only at this time of year, and sighed. Mostly because it brought back memories of lazy days outside sitting in my chair, slipping them on and off and revelling in the feel of the air around my feet and the grass between my toes as they were so easy to get on and off.

Min ordered, "Stop daydreaming about footwear, you weirdo." She thrust the peeler into my hand and said, "Work your magic."

I didn't need telling twice. While we prepped, I filled her in on everything and we speculated about what it meant. The death was clearly a conundrum, as how had it happened, but Maddie's, and even Roy's actions were questionable too. The dropped bucket was something that stuck with me, as it was almost like she'd done it on purpose. Did she want me out of the picture because she knew I'd been involved in other cases? Would she have murdered the DI once she'd dealt with me?

"You're sure it wasn't an accident?"

"No, not really. But she didn't seem concerned. Although, I can't see it being either of them."

"Me either, as it's risking their business."

"Let's just forget about it and enjoy ourselves. Isn't it time for a Baileys?"

"It's still only the morning."

"Wow. It feels like it's the afternoon. What a day it's been already."

"It sure has. Okay, let's have one. I do love the creamy taste. Every year I wonder why we only drink it at Christmas, and vow to buy some, then forget until the next year. It's weird."

"It makes it special."

Once the drinks were made, we sat next to Anxious, both of us squashed as he refused to budge and pretended to be fast asleep, and clinked glasses.

"Cheers," we said, and sipped.

"So good," Min sighed.

"The best."

As silence descended, our attention drifted to the presents.

"Should we?" I asked.

"I think we should. After the morning we've had, we deserve it."

"Max, I've been thinking."

"Yes?"

"That man was dressed as Father Christmas, right?"

"Sure."

"So maybe it was him who left the presents. Maybe, for whatever reason, he snuck into the van and left us gifts. After he did it, something happened and he was killed. I don't know how, or why, but it's possible, isn't it?"

"It's definitely possible. But why on earth would he do it? It makes no sense. Not that any of this does."

"That's where it gets tricky. I can't come up with a single reason why he'd leave presents, but someone did. I know this is very confusing, but in a weird kind of way it makes sense."

"Then maybe the best thing to do is to open them and see what's inside. That way, we'll know if the gifts were really for us or not. It could be that this was a mistake. A terrible, sad mistake."

"And the tree and presents are for someone else? The children in the van maybe? Have you seen them yet?"

"No."

"I bet that's it! The kids are missing out and we have their toys."

"I don't think teenagers want toys. They want computer games and new smartphones," I teased.

"Not the toddler! And anyway, that would still be weird. Either Santa's been hitting the booze too hard, or we're yet to figure out the real reason why someone snuck in and left us this stuff."

"Let's finish prepping for dinner, then we can open them. Sound good?"

"Definitely."

We got busy with the rest of the work, which didn't take long, and as we finished cleaning down the tiny counter and the fold-out table behind the passenger seat which we'd need for more space, we grinned at each other.

"Present time?" asked Min, her excitement building.

"Definitely." Then I recalled that I'd meant to remind Min earlier that we needed butter. We were out, and without it there was no way to get the potatoes and meat cooked how we liked them. "Um, Min, we need butter. The shop in the village is open, and they're bound to stock it, so I thought maybe we could go for a walk. Clear our heads and get some exercise. Anxious needs a you-know-what anyway, and let's be honest, without the gazebo set up and the outdoor kitchen, it's beyond cramped in here cooking and just trying to find a spot to sit. What do you say?"

"Oh, gosh, a million times yes! Max, I love the van, and I adore being here with you guys, but it's so tiny. It's fine for sleeping and spending a little time in, but cooking and living in here is a bit much. We definitely need the gazebo and cooking at the big table outside is so much easier. The moment the snow clears we have to set it up again. At least the table if it isn't broken. It's a shame about the damage, as otherwise we'd have a clear space outside to relax in."

"I know, and we should have checked the weather report last night. We could have sorted everything out. I think I was too excited about you being here, and it was fun snuggling down watching a movie with us together, but you're right, it's so cramped with the three of us. We'll get through this, then clear out the gazebo if the snow clears. But I'm assuming it will be here until it's time for you to leave. Think you can handle it this once?"

"Of course, and it's been good for us anyway. It lets us see what life would be like if…"

"If?" I prompted, my heart fluttering.

"If we live here together," she blurted, a flash of anger at being put on the spot, hands on hips, daring me to tease her.

I decided tact and downplaying my hopes were in order, so asked, "Are we going for a walk then?"

Anxious went from snoring to apoplectic with excitement, and launched off the bench seat then ran around in the tiny space, barking merrily, beyond keen for some exercise.

Min sniggered. "I don't think we have a choice now, do we? You said the W word on purpose, didn't you?"

"Me?" I protested, hiding my smirk by grabbing my coat and slipping it on.

"Yes, you. Right, let me go and get my wellies, then we can have a mini adventure."

While I finished tidying inside, not easy with a semi-feral dog running circuits around a sixties VW campervan as the track was very small, Min nipped out to retrieve her boots. She returned red in the face, covered in snow, and shivering.

"It's freezing out there. The temperature has dropped and the snow is starting to get a crust on it."

"Should have left your wellies in here," I gloated, pointing to mine. "Those beauties will be toasty. I bet yours are making your feet numb."

"And I got wet socks getting them. Maybe Crocs aren't the best after all."

"Not for snow, they aren't."

Min changed into dry socks then we wrapped up, put a festive jacket on Anxious, plus a cute scarf with a bell, and a hat with a pom-pom Min had picked up for him, and we were good to go.

The secluded area we were parked in looked so different without the snowman, and we wandered over then stood amid the piles of dirty, trampled snow and studied the various vehicles. Vee looked awesome, about as festive as a van could be. The large mystery motorhome was still devoid of life outside, the family van was loud with the noise of kids shouting and laughing, and the lone guy, Kev, could be heard banging pots and presumably preparing his dinner whilst swigging whisky. There was no sign of the DI, but I felt certain he was around somewhere.

Clarence's footprints trailed back and forth from each vehicle, but the owners clearly hadn't come out to talk to him beyond the threshold, just a few steps for the Transit, but the lack of footprints at the hidden motorhome meant either they weren't in when he called, or he'd gone inside to chat to them. Hopefully, we'd catch up later and I'd learn what he'd uncovered.

But my main focus was on my family, and how happy Min and Anxious were. We linked arms, laughed as Anxious jumped from footprint to footprint, and headed towards the exit.

With no signs of life at the static home, and the digger parked up, we assumed the owners were enjoying some quiet time while they could, doing their best to enjoy the day, so decided to leave them alone. After a short struggle to get over a massive pile of snow Maddie had inexplicably piled up at the end of the track, which would block any vehicles from entering or exiting, we were beyond relieved to get onto real ground with nothing but a thin fresh covering of snow that was melting as fast as it fell thanks to the heat absorbed by the gravel track.

The sun shone bright and cheery, and we both acknowledged that this was exactly what we needed. Anxious was in his element, dashing across the track as he followed scents, occasionally diving into drifts only to emerge with a head covered in snow and a snort to clear his nostrils.

Min and I laughed our way down the track, buoyed and energised by the beautiful day and pristine surroundings. What a truly stunning world this was, especially when you were with the ones you loved and the countryside dazzled you with its purity. I wondered what it would be like in a busy town with traffic kicking filthy slush onto the pavement, rather than here where everything was white and the air was clean. I could never go back to living in urban areas, of that I was convinced. I needed this open space, and knew without doubt that it affected my mental health in a positive way.

Hugging a tree and being grounded in nature might have been seen as nonsense when it got out of hand, but there was no denying the healing power of the natural world and the untold benefits I was reaping by travelling around in Vee, even though I was well aware of the contradictions as I lived in a vehicle belching fumes to live such a life.

Maddie had done a great job clearing the track, and I began to realise why she'd focused on it. With the high stone walls and hedges, most of it was in shade all day at this time of year, so it would take an age to melt, especially because of the drifts. At least this way it would be clear once main access routes had melted and the gritting trucks could get out.

After what felt like only a few minutes, but turned out to be half an hour, we got to the junction and turned left onto a larger road, but still little more than a wide track, and here we began to get unstuck. Thinking the main routes even in this remote area would have been cleared at least a little if by nothing more than farm vehicles compressing the snow, we were sorely mistaken.

The going was hard, and slow, with drifts over our knees, the temperature plummeting as we trudged along dark roads with overhanging trees blocking the light. Everything was in deep shadow, with only the crunch of our boots and the occasional bird call breaking the silence as we huffed and puffed, Anxious now in my arms as he was too small to make it on foot.

And then, like a miracle, we burst free from the gloom onto a clear road at a T-junction, with the small village directly ahead. Cars were few and far between, but there were signs of life. Most vehicles were congregated around the pub where cheery voices drifted on the still air, inviting and welcome. Smoke rose from the chimney, the smell a beautiful thing, and we hurried forward, kicking up slush but not caring, feeling like we'd emerged from the apocalypse into a new beginning.

Definitely time for a pint!

Chapter 10

"Whoah!"
"Eek!"
"Grr!"

Chapter 11

"Let's try again," I gasped, eyes raised expectantly in Min's direction, noting that all colour had drained from her face.

Anxious growled, hackles raised, as he brushed against my leg for protection.

All eyes turned to us, our outburst loud even above the din of the pub.

"I think we better," stammered Min, the colour returning as she calmed. She removed her hat and shook out her golden locks, causing me to gasp again as how lucky a guy was I, and the rest of the customers to do likewise. Min beamed at me then everyone else, then uncharacteristically she smiled as she waved and said, "Hi!" to the roomful of Santas.

"Ho, ho, ho," was the reply, this time causing me to blanch and wonder if I'd mistakenly drunk the water from that strange island in Cornwall on my last murder mystery adventure.

"Um, shall we get a drink?" I suggested, trying to ignore everyone.

"Make mine a double."

"A double pint?"

"No, a double of whatever's the strongest."

With Anxious brushing against my leg, and Min holding tight to my arm, we cautiously entered the pub properly, having been stuck just inside the door until now. The old-fashioned public house with low ceilings, thick oak beams, brass ornaments everywhere, and the walls covered in old photos was rammed with what I could best describe as a Father Christmas convention.

With at least fifty people or more inside, at least two-thirds of them were dressed in Santa outfits, a mix of mostly men but a few women in costume too.

There were even three Santas behind the bar, smiling happily and giving a festive "Ho, ho, ho," to everyone who ordered, be they a Santa or regular folks.

The way parted like a sea of red and white synthetic water, everyone smiling warmly, clearly happy to be out of the cold and close to the beer. As the door banged open behind us and yet more Santas appeared along with some regular looking locals, we were forgotten and everyone returned to gossiping and discussing how their Christmas had been so far.

We made it to the bar and were served by a woman of no more than twenty wearing a rather provocative interpretation of the traditional outfit, with a low-cut red and white fur-lined jacket with the sleeves cut off, and a hat at a jaunty angle. She smiled warmly and asked what we'd like, so I had a pint of cider and Min went for a large glass of Prosecco.

Once I'd paid, I simply had to ask. "What's the deal with the Father Christmas costumes?"

"Isn't it incredible? It's the same every year. All the locals dress up and come to the pub before their dinner. Everyone compares costumes and has a drink to celebrate another year. It's so sweet. This is my first year working here, but I'm definitely going to keep the job now. I love it!" The barmaid beamed at us, clearly waiting for us to agree.

"Really cool," said Min, nudging me when I didn't respond.

"Yes, it's a fun idea. But why do they do it?"

"Tradition," grunted a rosy-cheeked man beside us. "It goes back to the war when rationing was in place. Everyone would come to the pub to have a natter and get out of the house, and people began to dress up. But there weren't many options back then, so somebody had the idea to dress as Father Christmas. It stuck, and now the village does it every year."

"I see. So it's not for any real reason?"

"It's Christmas," he said with a frown of confusion. "What more reason do you need?" He took a deep pull on his pint then turned his attention back to the group of men he'd been talking with.

"Fun, eh?" asked the barmaid with a wink.

"Sure. Excuse me, I don't suppose you know if anyone's missing who should be here today, do you?"

"Missing? How'd you mean? Like usually comes? I wouldn't know. Someone might. Shall I ask?" Before I had a chance to protest, she called out in a surprisingly loud voice, "Hey, everyone, this guy wants to know if anyone's missing who should be here. Is there?"

With so much attention on us, I felt uncomfortable, and realised this was a terrible idea. The locals clearly hadn't heard about the murder, as why would they have unless the DI had been to talk to people, and now we were in a rather awkward position.

"Who wants to know?" someone called out.

"Why would anyone be missing?"

"Has something happened?"

"Whose dog is this stealing my crisps?"

Min rushed off to retrieve Anxious, clearly pleased to have the excuse, so now I was the centre of attention and squirming.

Thinking on my feet, I simply said, "It just seems like a lot of Santas, so I was making a joke that maybe there should be a few more. Sorry, as you were."

There were a few grumbles and head shakes, but everyone lost interest in me and returned to drinking and chatting.

Except the guy I'd already spoken to.

"Why did you make up that excuse? I heard what you asked Mary, and that's a very specific question. Where are you from?" He leaned close until his thick white beard tickled my nose, and peered into my eyes. "What are you hiding?"

Laughing nervously, I said, "Me? Nothing. Why?"

"Because, like I said, that's a very specific question. Where are you from? You aren't local."

"We're camping at the site up the hill. Well, not camping. I have a VW."

"On Christmas Day? Pull the other one. As if! Everyone is at home today. How can you do dinner otherwise? How would Santa come?"

"He already came last night."

Getting right up in my face again and peering into my eyes solemnly, he asked, "Did he? Did he really?"

"Er, yes."

"Then that's alright then," he giggled, slapping me on the back and downing the dregs of his pint. He called for another and was served in seconds, then demanded, "Now, what's this about? Why did you ask if someone was missing?"

"No reason," I said, knowing it sounded utterly lame. "Nothing really. It's not my place to say."

"Now I'm intrigued. Something has happened, hasn't it? You can tell me. I won't say a word." He leaned in closer, and so did five other guys who had been eavesdropping, and as Min returned with a grinning Anxious, crisp bits all over his snout, the rest of the pub seemed to pick up on our conversation and theirs slowly died until all focus was back on us.

"Honestly, it's nothing. We just fancied a walk from the campsite. The snow is so thick up there, but Maddie cleared the track, so we figured we'd come and pick up some butter from the shop, then saw the pub."

"Don't take us for fools," someone shouted.

"Yeah, what's your game?" screeched a woman.

"He's up to no good," grumbled a man.

"Shame on you," hissed the barmaid, smiling and winking at me. "Sorry, I got caught up in the excitement. What's going on?"

"It's nothing. Please let us enjoy our drinks in peace."

Everyone protested, but when I refused to say any more they eventually returned to the business of getting merry and we took the opportunity to grab a seat in the corner out of their way.

We huddled close together, heads almost touching, and took a nervous sip of our drinks. Anxious settled on the floor after checking for crumbs, sorely disappointed.

"That was a close call," whispered Min. "What did you say to them?"

"Only what you heard. I made a mistake and asked if any Santas were missing. The old guy figured I knew something and badgered me, then everyone else joined in. I shouldn't have asked. It's not our place to break the news of a murder. Especially today."

"I'm amazed nobody has heard about it yet. Shouldn't the police have warned the locals?"

"No police have arrived yet. The roads are impassable. And clearly Clarence hasn't been back down here to ask questions."

"Max, there's a high chance the man we found is from the village and he might be a regular in here. Maybe we should tell them."

"But then we give away the element of surprise. I'm not sure that's a good idea. In fact, I'm not sure what to do. What do you think?"

"That you're probably right and we should keep quiet. Maybe someone will let something slip. But then again, maybe they won't. With so many people dressed up, would they even know if a few men who usually come aren't here? It can't be the same people every year, can it?"

"Doubtful. Min, this is weird, right? It isn't just me, is it?"

"Definitely not. It's odd, but lots of villages have their own traditions and I guess this is theirs."

"The guy at the bar said it's just something they've done every year since the war. A way to celebrate and have a knees-up."

"I bet the dead man is a local. Someone must be missing him. Maybe there's a missing persons report by now and we can find out who he is."

"Could be."

"When we go back up, we'll have to find Clarence and ask him. Max, everyone keeps looking at us."

I took a peek and Min was right. We were definitely being watched and people were clearly gossiping. "Maybe we should go. Drink up."

We hurried through our drinks, which was a shame as the cider was lovely and Min was enjoying her bubbly, but when you can't relax it takes the enjoyment out of it, and this was of our own doing anyway.

I returned the glasses to the bar to save the staff the trouble, and hurried outside to meet Min and Anxious before I got asked any more questions.

No sooner had the door swung shut behind me than the man from the bar hurried out, wrapping his Santa jacket around him and shivering.

"It's cold enough to freeze the knickers off a donkey," he grumbled.

"What about horses?" I asked.

"Oh yes, cold enough for them too," he cackled, then began hacking. When he'd recovered, he asked, "Are you going to tell me what's going on?"

"I'm sorry, but we can't," said Min. "It's an awkward situation, but it isn't our place to say anything."

"Fair enough, and I can't imagine what the issue might be, but if you're asking if someone is missing then I can only assume that someone actually is missing. Right?"

"Like Min said, we can't say."

"Right you are. So, although you guys are winding me up, I'll tell you. There are three men who should be here but aren't. They live alone like me. Guys who have been here for years. No family, nothing to do at Christmas apart from come for a few pints, and they are always here. This year they aren't."

"Have you called them?"

"We aren't friendly like that. We're drinking buddies now and then, but not real friends. Just pub mates when we bump into each other, which is most days," he added, looking guilty. "Don't even know their numbers or anything like that. But I do know where they live. I was going to go check on them. Want to come?"

"How old are they? No offence, but are they your age?"

"Old duffers, you mean? Actually, one's my age, the other two are thirty or forty or some stupid young number. Loners, you might call them. They work hard and then come straight to the pub after work. Christmas is tough for a lot of us, so we're always here. They do a fine roast dinner on Christmas Day and we always eat together. There's about twenty of us who eat here, but three are missing. Nobody has heard from them or seen them since yesterday. They should be here."

"Then we should go and check it out. I'm sure everything is fine, but it's best to be sure." Min smiled at the man and he clearly warmed to her.

He moved closer, straightened his jacket, and mumbled, "You're so pretty."

"Thank you. That's sweet. I'm Min. This is Max. And that's Anxious." As the man frowned, Min added hurriedly, "It's his name, not his emotional state."

"Ah, okay," he said, clearly confused. "Oh, I'm Frank."

We shook, then followed Frank through the village, mindful of the time. I was getting twitchy as there was no way we'd be eating dinner any time soon now. Nothing was even on a slow cook as it was too risky to leave unattended, and it was closing in on midday now. I supposed we'd eat in the evening instead and just have something light for a late lunch. It was turning out to be a very different Christmas than usual.

The village was home to only five hundred residents, so it took literally a few minutes to get to the first house. Frank knocked and we waited for an answer which never came, our concerns growing. He knocked again, and this time someone called out then answered the door.

Turned out the guy had lost track of time, meaning he'd gone heavy on the morning drinking and fallen asleep. We cut the conversation short as otherwise they would have been nattering for ages, but his buddy promised to be around at the pub soon.

It was a similar story at the other two houses. Both men had crashed out, clearly feeling low because of being alone, so had hit it hard and early.

With time getting on, we said our farewells to Frank after seeing him back to the pub as the pavements were treacherous and the roads even worse as everything began to ice over.

Finally alone, we hurried to the small corner shop and grabbed the butter then paid the cashier before braving the elements and stepping out into a snowstorm that had sprung up from nowhere while we were inside.

"What now?" asked Min.

"We go back and see what Clarence has found out. Unless you have any other ideas?"

"I feel like we should be figuring out who the man is. He must be from around here, surely?"

"I'm not so sure. He could be from anywhere. Remember his notebook?"

"Sure."

"If he's a builder, he might have been working on someone's property and is from another town or village. Could be twenty or more miles away."

"True, but is that what your gut is telling you? Because mine is saying he's from this village and if we ask enough questions we'll find out who it is."

"Min, I'm sure you're right, but it's Christmas Day and we can't go knocking on everyone's door to ask if someone is missing. I'm sure that if someone is, they'll have been reported to the police and Clarence or someone else will visit them."

"Unless it's someone who lives alone. Who will report them missing then?"

"You're right, but I'm convinced the answer to the mystery lies back at the campsite. Don't ask me why, but that's how I feel."

"Then we better get back there."

"You okay with that? I know it's tough to figure out what to do, and I could happily stay in the pub and see what turns up, but we have to respect the police and let them do their jobs too. There's trying to help, and then there's interfering and scaremongering. It isn't our place to put the whole village into panic mode on today of all days. It's a worry, for sure, and we don't want anything bad to happen to anyone else, but is it down to us?"

"Absolutely not, and you're right. I don't want to freak everyone out. But I also know that if it was me I'd want to know if someone was killed. People can take precautions then. What if it's someone singling out those who are alone?"

"I know. It's awful. What should we do then? I'm happy to go along with whatever you decide."

"No way are you making me pick! I don't want to make the wrong decision and interfere in a police investigation. Clarence knows best, I think we can agree on that, so let's discuss it with him and take it from there."

"Good call. I agree. Come on, before this snow gets too deep to make it back home."

Arm in arm, and feeling the bite of an icy wind get into our bones, we hurried through the deserted streets of the village, the only sounds coming from the pub or the occasional pedestrian knocking on the door of family then being ushered inside cosy houses where lights shone, fires burned, and children squealed for joy.

The decorations strung up along the high street sparkled in the sunshine, but as we turned the corner and headed back up towards the campsite, the cheer was gone, replaced with the gloom of the overhanging trees. Our mood turned sombre and we were silent until we broke free of the cloying atmosphere and the sun once again hit our faces.

It was with a great sense of relief that we made it to the cleared track, and with a sweat building thanks to the exertion, we marched up the hill, Anxious yipping at our ankles, keen to get into the warm.

But that would have to wait as we were confronted with something that convinced us this day would remain far from peaceful.

Chapter 12

"No! It can't be!" wailed Min, burrowing into my chest as we halted.

"I can't believe it's another body. I was sure the killing was a one-off." I stroked Min's head through her hat but it was small comfort, I knew. Cautiously, I edged forward once she'd recovered from the shock a little, and approached the body in the lane, literally a minute or two away from the campsite.

A thick blanket covered the corpse, but it was still obvious it was a body and not just a pile of junk. For a start, legs stuck out, and the shape was unmistakable.

Min reached out and grabbed my hand then yanked me back. "Max, don't get any closer. The killer might be watching and ready to pounce." She glanced around, full of fear, but the track was clear and the hedges too dense and high for anyone to be lurking, ready to ambush.

"There's nobody here. We're safe. At least for now. Wait here. I need to take a look."

"Just be careful, and I'm coming too."

Anxious looked at me then Min, before trotting over, tail up, ears primed, then wagged as he approached.

"That's weird. Normally, he's good at picking up on the vibe. He should be growling with his tail down," I noted, perplexed by his actions. When he began sniffing at the body then licking the blanket, I was utterly confounded.

"He isn't scared at all. Anxious, come here." Min patted her thighs and Anxious turned, head cocked, confused by her call. He scurried over then sat, waiting for us to tell him it was okay to merrily sniff a corpse.

"What is it, boy? Do you know the person?" I asked.

Anxious woofed in the affirmative, then turned and scampered back over and pawed at the blanket.

"I guess we need to take a look," I sighed, wishing we could go home and begin cooking.

As a team, we inched forward, two of us wary, one of us enjoying the game. We stood over the body, then just to get it over with I bent and whipped off the blanket and jumped back, although I wasn't sure why. The dead couldn't hurt me, but I was jittery and worried about what I might see.

Min shrieked, "It's Clarence!" and gripped my arm.

"Someone's murdered the DI!" I gasped, not quite believing it.

Anxious barked, the tone not what I'd expected, almost happy, then he cast a disapproving glance our way before licking Clarence's bloody face.

Min gripped my arm tight and I almost jumped out of my skin as Clarence convulsed then shot upright and groaned as he rubbed at his temple where blood was oozing from a gash to his forehead.

"You're not dead," gushed Min, exhaling sharply.

"I hope not, although I feel like I should be." Clarence moved his hand in front of his face and inspected the blood, then shrugged before attempting to stand. He collapsed back down onto the soaking ground. "Went dizzy. Give me a moment. Can you help me up?"

"Is that wise? Shouldn't you rest?"

"I'm fine. Just a bump."

"What happened?" I offered a hand and Clarence took it and I hauled him to his feet, the wound clearly not too serious, but the blood plentiful.

"I got attacked. By Santa. I have to go. He went that way." Clarence pointed down the lane.

"We didn't see anyone."

"Then they must have clambered over the wall and gone into the fields, but they were definitely heading towards the village. I need to get after them. I can't believe I let myself get ambushed. One moment I was walking towards the village as I figured I'd better break the news and start asking around, and the next thing I knew Santa sprang off that wall," he pointed to a lower collapsed section about shoulder height, "and swung what looked like a club at me. Probably just a tree branch, but it really hurts. I blacked out, I guess. Where did this blanket come from? Why was it on me?"

"No idea. We found you with it. Clarence, are you okay? That's a nasty cut you've got, and the lump is getting bigger as we speak. Maybe you need to go to the hospital."

"I'm fine. And no way would we make it anyway. I just heard from the station and they can't get anyone out here any time soon. I'm on my own, and most likely it will remain that way until tomorrow. Look, thanks for helping, but I gotta go." Clarence carefully felt his bump and winced, then squared his shoulders, patted his pocket where his hip flask resided but shook his head, trying to avoid the booze, then began walking down the hill.

"Clarence, you can't just go!" called Min. "You were attacked. What if you collapse?"

"I'm fine! I told you. I've been on the job for decades, and have never let anyone get the better of me before. No way will I let this guy get away with it."

We hurried after him as he waved over his shoulder and continued marching toward the village, and I pulled him to a stop. "It was definitely a man? Did you see his face?"

"No. He had a full Santa outfit on, including a thick fake beard, and his hat was low over his eyes. But he wore sunglasses and I think he even had padding. The way he moved was like he was a thin man, but his stomach was bulked out. I bet it was the blanket he covered me with."

"Did he try to kill you? What happened after he attacked?" asked Min.

"He jumped down, didn't make a sound, and swung the club at me. I was too late trying to defend myself and fell after the first blow. Knocked me out cold. He must have heard you guys and ran off. Not sure why he put the blanket over me. That's rather odd."

"Very," I agreed. "And why attack you anyway? What was the point?"

"To stop me looking into this, of course!" he snapped. "Sorry, I didn't mean to shout. I'm rattled, is all. Sorry, but I have to go. You get back to the site and lock yourselves in. Don't take any risks, and do not try to deal with this yourselves. This is important. I'm new to the village, been here less than a year, but I need to tell people about the death and see if anyone's missing. There are no reports of a missing person yet, which is odd as most folks are at home today, but I need to ask around and try to get a handle on things. The longer it goes on, the less chance of finding the killer. And besides, I bet he's heading to the village. He might kill again, so I have to go." With a nod, Clarence ran down the lane, his speed surprising us.

"We need to follow him," I told Min. "He doesn't know what he's letting himself in for."

"He lives here, so should know quite a few locals."

"He just said he's been here less than a year. He won't know who to trust or where to start. We haven't even told him what we've been up to and we haven't heard if he's spoken to everyone at the campsite. Plus, what if he collapses? His head was a mess."

"Then let's go!" Min sprinted off, which caused my stress levels to soar instantly as who knew where the killer was lurking?

"Anxious, look after Min."

Like a shot, he was off, tearing after her, barking for her to wait up, but Min was focused and I doubt she even heard him as her hat was over her ears and the blood would be pumping.

With no choice, I gave chase, mindful of the slippery track as the snow fell and ice hid beneath the powdery coating. I soon discovered that running in wellies was not easy. Even though they were expensive and a perfect fit, it felt awkward and constricting on my calves, and I didn't have the right freedom in my ankles, but Min seemed to be coping absolutely fine and had a good head start I was struggling to shorten.

Thankfully, she glanced behind and slowed to wait for me, so I caught up and we ran side-by-side the rest of the way, no ability to chat as the air was so cold and dry that it seemed to suck the breath right out of me. My face stung, we slipped repeatedly, but we didn't stop as Clarence was now in sight and flagging, allowing us to close the gap.

Anxious took the lead and easily matched the DI's pace, barking at him to wait up so we could join him. But Clarence ignored his calls, seemingly focused on catching his attacker and putting this case to rest, and all in time for dinner.

At the junction, we finally closed the gap and, with a nod from Clarence we crossed over and entered the village. People were out in force, going in and out of houses now it was dinner time, bearing gifts, laughing, joking, or arguing like the rest of the country would be doing about now, everyone looking forward to a sumptuous feast and a few drinks before watching the TV and settling for some over-the-top drama on Eastenders or listening to the usual speech.

For us, there would be none of that as we were on the trail of a murderer, and the DI was intent on catching his man.

He gasped as he caught sight of a man in full Santa costume, and sped off, determined to catch his man.

"He's going to come a cropper if he keeps racing around like that. The roads are like an ice rink," I noted, proving it by skidding along the edge and almost breaking a hip as I slipped.

"Careful. I get it. No need to show off! Come on, we need to help him out. He's convinced that man is the killer, but there's no way to know."

"He hasn't seen what we've seen," I sighed, managing to right myself then taking it carefully as we moved as fast as we dared along the treacherous pavement covered in slush and ice.

Clarence was having difficulties as he slipped and slid along ahead of us, following the Santa who entered the pub. We caught up with him just before the harried DI was about to go in, and Min grabbed his arm.

"There's something we need to tell you about the pub," insisted Min, trying to pull him away.

"You should listen to her," I told him.

"In a minute. The guy's just gone inside, so we have our man. I'll give him what for. Killing poor people and attacking detectives means he's going down." With a grim grunt, and brushing himself down, Clarence shook free of Min then shoved the door open and marched inside.

With no other choice apart from to leave him to fend for himself, we followed right behind.

"I'm looking for Santa," bellowed DI Clarence Carroll. "Has anyone seen a man dressed as Father Christmas? He's…" The DI's words trailed off as the room went deathly silent and fifty plus Santas turned to gawp at him.

"Um, there's something you should know," I said with a cheesy grin as the room erupted into pandemonium and the DI blanched.

Clarence did a double-take of the room, then me, then Min, and even Anxious. The little guy grinned and barked, causing the room to once again fall silent as everyone focused on Clarence as he removed his hat and scratched at his head, wincing as he inadvertently caught his wound.

"Why are you all dressed as Father Christmas? Where is the man who just came in? I demand to know."

"Who is this guy?" shouted a Santa.

"He's that newcomer," a woman answered. Again, dressed as Santa.

"Clarence, I warned you about drinking too much," hollered the barmaid we'd met earlier. "Are you having an episode? Have you had a rough day?"

"Yes, I've had a rough day," he griped, glancing at me. "I'll tell you about it in a minute. But first, I want to know who just entered. I'm chasing a suspect and he's dressed as Father Christmas. He just came in." Clarence studied the crowd then sighed; he was clearly fighting a losing battle. "I need a drink," he grumbled, then, ignoring everyone, headed towards the bar.

"Um, I was the last one in, I think. Just got here." A merry looking Santa with a large belly that was clearly genuine, and about five six and at least seventy stepped from a small group and barred the DI's way. "What did you want to ask me?"

"No, not you. It must have been someone else. And someone please explain what is going on here?"

"It's Christmas!" the entire pub chorused, then laughed as Noddy Holder echoed the words through blaring speakers and everyone began to jig about in the confined space.

Overwhelmed, Clarence pushed through the revellers and made it to the bar. We followed, ready to help if he needed it, which I was sure he would soon enough. With a pint already in his hand, he sipped and let his shoulders relax, a no-man's land around him as he was likely to blow at any moment.

"You good?" I asked, me taking one side, Min the other, Anxious on the prowl for crisps.

"Yes, I'm good. Do you know what's happening? I'm not hallucinating, am I?"

"No, we just came from here but you didn't give us the chance to explain. Apparently, they dress like this very year. It's a tradition. I guess if this is your first year here, you've never seen it before, although they seem to know you."

"I might come in for a pint a few times a month," he mumbled, draining half his beer in a single gulp.

"More like every other night!" said the barmaid. She leaned over then asked, "You okay? What's going on? You look awful. And what happened to your head? Have you been drinking too much? I know it must be hard, what with moving to a new place and being alone, but you still need to watch it."

"No, I haven't been drinking. At least, nothing but a sip. There's been an incident and nobody else can make it, so it's down to me." With a final gulp, he downed his pint then asked, "Another please."

"That's not a good idea," I warned. "Especially with your bump to the head. Never mind that you have an investigation."

"You're right. Once I get a taste, I can't stop. Best not to have another."

"What investigation?" asked the barmaid, eyes locked on Clarence. "Come on, you can tell me. Do we need to be concerned?"

The room had grown quiet. Not silent, but people were obviously trying to eavesdrop. Clarence noticed, so with a sigh he turned to face everyone. "There's been a murder. A man dressed as Father Christmas. Just like you lot."

The assembled patrons gasped, then erupted into raucous chatter, before Clarence raised a hand for silence. Nobody took any notice until the barmaid shouted, "Shut it, you lot!"

The room fell silent immediately. She might have been new to the job, and very young, but everyone clearly knew that she meant business.

"I need to know if anyone's missing, and I need to know if anyone knows of any local builders matching the description I'm about to give you."

"Not many builders who dress as Santa," someone joked, only to receive a communal boo for such bad taste.

"Everyone settle down and please try to think if anyone's missing or if anything strange has happened lately. I know this is a shock, and the last thing I want to do is ruin your special day, but obviously this is important. I just got attacked and the man ran towards the village, so if anyone knows anything please tell me. If it's okay, I'll be in the back room, so you can come and see me in private. It's totally confidential, but we do need to find this person." With a nod to a man behind the bar who I assumed was the owner, Clarence marched to the right then through an open doorway, leaving the punters shocked and silent.

Min tugged at my arm so we made our escape. As the door clanged closed behind us, the pub erupted with noise as the speculations and questions grew louder.

"He's got his work cut out for him in there," said Min.

"I don't think he'll have much luck though. I'm not even convinced the victim is from here."

"What makes you think that? The most likely answer is he's a local and someone killed him then for whatever reason decided to stow the body up at the campsite."

"But that's the problem. Why on earth would anyone go to that kind of trouble? The snow would have already been quite thick, so how would they even get him up there then into the field? Then they had to build the snowman. No, I think something else entirely is going on here."

"Like what?"

With a nervous laugh, I admitted, "I have absolutely no idea."

Min smiled in sympathy then linked her arm through mine and we headed back home once again.

Chapter 13

We made it back to Vee eventually, but it wasn't easy. Just as we were about to open up, I caught movement from the corner of my eye and spotted a woman with long blond hair hanging below her woollen hat dash from the facilities block and towards the family vehicle. I was in two minds about whether to go and talk to Sam's wife, but figured it could wait as I really wanted to get dinner on. We'd already missed so much of the day and now it would be evening before we ate our main meal, so had to not only get going with cooking the meat and finishing prepping, but we had to make lunch too.

By the time I'd made up my mind, the mystery woman had already gone inside. It was a joy to get out of our wellies and the layers, but we were boiling from the exertion, although I turned the heater on anyway. With the solar useless, I was relying on the electrical hookup to keep the leisure battery topped up, something I'd hardly used since I first began my new life, and somehow it felt like cheating. I'd wanted to be totally independent, but even with my expensive power bank that held some serious juice, it wouldn't last running the heater, so accepted that sometimes I'd have to use mains. I needed to investigate the diesel heaters most vanlifers now used, but that would be for another day and probably when the weather was better so I could either figure out how to do it myself or leave it with a garage and camp for a night or two.

But right now, we had more important things to contend with. Time to cook. Determined not to be put completely out of kilter by the killing and general weirdness going on, I insisted Min relax and put her feet up, so she and Anxious did exactly that and chilled on the bench seat. It didn't leave me much room, as whenever I moved I'd bump into her legs until she shifted position and actually did put her feet up, but I soon got into the zone and began to get creative with dinner. I had to pop out a few times and rummage through the snow to retrieve items from the storage boxes outside, and cleared away what I could of the gazebo carcass, but left most of it as I was so cold.

How did you cook Christmas Dinner with all the trimmings when you had no oven, no spacious outdoor kitchen, and nowhere to light a fire to cook on? I wished I had the gazebo, but I'd have to make do with what I did have available and that was a gas hob built into the counter next to the sink and a spare portable double ring cooker that took a small bottle. I braved the elements once again and retrieved that, whilst I thought about what I could actually cook, my previous plans out of the frost-covered window.

"Ah, I know," I blurted, causing Min and Anxious to glance up from their Kindles, eyebrows raised.

"Problem?" asked Min.

"No, I was just thinking how to make dinner, then had an epiphany. Do you mind if we do something less traditional? I was going to get all the gas rings going and try my best to do a roast, but that's not one-pot cooking, is it?"

"Not exactly. I assumed you wanted to make a roast, but I'm happy with anything. To be honest, I think you should do a one-pot wonder. It's your tradition and what we always have."

"You're right, and that's what I'd decided. It won't be what we're used to on Christmas, but it should still be nice. So, you're up for it?"

"Of course.

"Then I'm going to do it. It might not be exactly by the rules, but I've got an idea and hopefully it will turn out great."

Min smiled, which lifted my spirits. She was so trusting when it came to my culinary quirks, and I knew that she would be happy with whatever I served. It wasn't just about the food, it was the trust, the love, the acceptance that this was what I enjoyed and she was content to leave me to it and was always grateful for whatever I dished up.

In my element, I figured out my recipe, checked the timings, then began. With so much food already prepped, although now I had to make a few changes, it didn't take too long before I was up and running with my modified menu. Once the kitchen was wiped down, I pulled out a bottle of Prosecco from the tiny fridge and popped the cork.

"Are we celebrating?" Min cast a lidded eye my way whilst Anxious didn't even stir from her lap—He'd given up on reading as it had made him too sleepy.

"We are. Being together, being alive, warm, and toasty in Vee, and that it's a beautiful world no matter what horrible things happen. Here's to us."

I passed Min her glass and we clinked, then smiled as we sipped, about as content as two people could be in a van stuck in a snowstorm with a dead Santa not far away and a field full of strange people. All of that faded away until it was just the three of us cocooned in the warm, if rather cramped, womb of Vee.

Min scooted up and we sat, grinning, as we enjoyed our wine.

"This is nice. Cramped, but nice." Min winked and I laughed, as why wouldn't I?

"It really is. Look, I know it's tiny, and it's nigh on impossible to get anything done in here, and cooking with no space and no counter is not what I'd call ideal, but you do like it, don't you?" I felt genuinely nervous, worried that this latest trip was a step too far, and Min would realise there was no way she could handle living like this for months through the bleakest British weather.

"Max, relax. It's all good. You're right about all of that, but it doesn't matter, and in fact, I think it's kind of cool."

"You do?"

"Sure. It's a different life. I mean, utterly different," she laughed, reaching out to touch first one side of the van, then leaning the other way past me and rapping on the door. "Yes, it's tiny, yes, it's annoying always getting in each other's way, but this is just a part of the life, and I truly enjoy it. It's living differently, learning to be more mindful of the other person, and what I am really enjoying is getting away from so much stuff. It's incredible how many things we own. I have a house full and it's just me. This teaches you what's important and to let go of so much that you don't need. One thing you can count on is that when I get back I'm going to have a proper sort out and sell a load of useless stuff."

"And why would you sell things?" I hinted with a raised eyebrow, sipping my drink to hide my wry smile.

"Never you mind about that. Drink up, as we do have a murder to solve. I hope Clarence is alright."

"He's a seasoned pro. He'll be fine." My heart pounded as I anticipated getting back out into the snow and trying to figure out this peculiar mystery. I definitely had the bug, and was itching to get this solved or at least find something to lead us in the right direction.

"I hope the Santas aren't giving him too much grief. The poor man looked ready to collapse when he saw them in the pub."

"His expression was priceless," I giggled, picturing his reaction. "He thought he had the culprit cornered, then was faced with a room full of half-hammered Father Christmases."

"You shouldn't laugh," giggled Min, nudging me with her elbow.

"I know. Let's hope he's seeing the funny side of it. It's a difficult job that he does, and having to explain to everyone what happened won't be easy. Especially because they'll want the gossip, but will be keen to get home for their dinner."

"I'm sure he can handle it. Although, his drinking is an issue. What did he say to you about it?"

"Not much, but he's clearly trying to handle it. Poor guy's alone and that must be tough. Maybe he'll show up later. Hope so. He seems nice. A hard nut to crack, but a decent guy. It's great having the detective on side rather than having to try to stay out of his way."

"It definitely makes a change. Right, come on, time to get busy."

"Doing what?"

"Max, in case you've forgotten, we still haven't spoken to that Sam guy's wife or children. And we have the mystery motorhome too. Should we check on that lone man? Kev, wasn't it? The one who stank of booze?"

"We could check in on him, sure. He's having a real hard time of things. I'm not sure what the problem is, but he's trying to get away from something. Maybe he wants to be alone?"

"On Christmas? He'll be getting hammered if his breath was anything to go by. He might want some company."

"Or he might have come here because that's the opposite of what he wants. First, let's see how Sam and his family are doing. Hopefully, they've been having a fun day. It's still weird the kids haven't been out to play though. Children always love snow."

"It's different now to when we were young. Parents worry more about bad things happening, and the children want to play with tech."

"True, but it's snow! Everyone loves it."

We finished our drinks, the warmth from the alcohol welcome as it fortified us for our foray outside, but I knew we needed sustenance as dinner would be hours, so knocked us up a very non-traditional cheese sandwich, which we had a veritable mountain of. Why did everyone, including me and Min, buy so much cheese at Christmas? It always ended up sitting in the fridge for weeks, until the very thought of another stale cracker and a slice of something fancy with blue veins sent a shiver down my spine. The pickle was lovely, though, and we had a few cheeky chocolates and some biscuits to finish it off, because it was Christmas after all, then we cleaned up and prepared to leave.

Looking like merry mummies escaped from a frosty tomb, we roused Anxious then exited. Once again, the snowstorm had returned with a vengeance. It seemed like we were heading for trouble, as according to the weather report that had finally updated to at least slightly reflect the reality, the storm would intensify for a few hours before passing to the east and giving us a brief spell of clear skies.

Already early afternoon, we literally had a few hours before it would be dark, but at least there was finally some hope on the horizon. With the shortest day behind us, from here on out we would get a few minutes of extra daylight every day and soon enough spring would be here and slowly I could ease back into the routines I'd enjoyed so much when I first began this life.

I practically salivated at the thought of returning to Crocs and cut-offs, sitting out in the sunshine and watching the world go by. It couldn't come soon enough.

"It isn't summer yet," laughed Min, wrapping her scarf around her neck another time and shivering.

"Are you reading my mind?"

"Maybe. Or maybe I just know that look you get. All wistful, and you kept staring at your feet. You and your Crocs. If you could wear them every day you would."

"True. And now you're a convert too."

"Only for indoor slippers. Not to be seen in public!"

Our mirth died as we glanced over at the mystery motorhome, but we turned away, deciding without speaking that we should visit Sam and his family first to check on things and then call on Kev to make sure he was alright. Of course, none of it was our responsibility, but with the owners seemingly taking a backseat to everything that was going on, we felt it was our duty to keep an eye on everyone without interfering.

With coats buttoned and zipped, scarves acting as mufflers, hats pulled low, dogs cuddled, and feet already freezing, we bowed our heads and hoped for the best. It became obvious immediately that the storm meant business. The snow was coming right at us almost sideways, blasting our ruddy cheeks with ice and freezing gales as we hunched over. The crunch of the old snow as it froze at least gave us something semi-solid to walk on, but the going was tough and by the time we reached the family van we were shivering and in need of a hot chocolate. Preferably with a generous sprinkling of marshmallows and maybe a Baileys top-up to really get the blood flowing.

Sam's awning had broken and sunk into the snow— nothing could repair it and it would need replacing, but it was pointless trying to do anything in this weather. The chunky Rhino roof rack looked like a giant sledge sat atop the motorhome, and the bike rack with the bikes had vanished beneath a mountainous drift. All the windows still had the tiny curtains drawn, presumably to keep the heat in, but we could still hear the family inside laughing and joking like they were on a loop. At least they were enjoying themselves. Christmas jingles blared from speakers, and I was surprised they could listen to them over and over like that, but then the whole set-up seemed repetitive. They were definitely a bunch of van lovers and the children clearly enjoyed themselves, most likely playing with whatever Santa had brought them.

I rapped on the door, stomping my feet to stop them freezing solid, with Min cuddled into me, making me decide that I actually enjoyed the conditions.

"One minute," shouted Sam. The noise died down a little, although the children continued to laugh and joke and his wife sang along to Mariah Carey belting out a song about snow and not needing any presents.

Sam opened the door just enough to peer through, then smiled when he realised it was us.

"Sorry, but you can't be too careful." He lowered his baseball bat and grinned, then eased through the door and closed it, slipping into his wellies, seemingly uncaring that he'd soaked his thick socks.

"We wanted to check you were all okay. How is your wife and the children? Are they coping alright?"

"Yes, fine. The little one's having some lunch, so excuse Jo if she doesn't come to say hello. The kids are still buzzing about their gifts, and we're going to have our dinner soon. How are you doing?"

"We're good. Cold, but good."

Sam clearly didn't take the hint and kept his back to the door, probably not wanting to disrupt family time by inviting us in. I assumed it was cramped enough inside anyway, and it would be a squeeze.

"So, any news?"

We filled him in on recent events and he was stunned but had nothing to offer but sympathy. After a quick chat, and a promise to let him know if anything else happened, we said our goodbyes then trudged back the way we'd come then veered off from our tracks towards Kev's fancy Transit with the nice attached tent.

"Did that seem weird to you?" asked Min.

"The fact his wife never says hello and the children don't want to play in the snow? Yes, a bit. But he's just being cautious, and I bet his wife wants to be left alone to enjoy the day."

"They sure laugh a lot, so he must be doing something right."

"True. And let's face it, today isn't exactly the best day for getting out and about."

"It's the worst," laughed Min.

"I wonder what they got for Christmas. Hope it wasn't new bikes."

"Very funny! I bet they're having a lovely time. It's nice that they're happy being together and enjoying themselves. Did you see the baseball bat though?"

"He's being cautious. That's a good idea."

"I suppose. Now, let's see how Kev is. I hope he won't be trouble."

"He seemed alright. He's got issues, but I think he'll be able to handle things."

"Then let's see, shall we?"

Chapter 14

We shouted above the hard sleet pummelling the tent as we approached, which I was surprised was still standing. Luckily, Kev had chosen a design with a decent pitch on the roof and had obviously been coming out regularly to scrape off the snow so it didn't get too heavy. Piles either side confirmed this, so he couldn't have been hitting the bottle too hard. Kev clearly knew what he was doing being a vanlifer for a few years, so had been through several winters and had adjusted his set-up accordingly.

This was what I loved about this life. Learning from others, stealing, or ahem, borrowing ideas, and I lamented not having thought more about the gazebo arrangement as I truly missed my outdoor kitchen and wished I'd invested in something more rugged. We live and learn, and there was nothing wrong with that. After all, this life was new to me and I'd vowed to not be discouraged by any mistakes I made as the only way to figure it out was to live through it then make changes.

"Hey," beamed Kev as he unzipped the tent, a blast of warm air greeting us like a slap in the face with a hot water bottle.

"Hi. We wanted to check in on you to see how you were doing." Min beamed at Kev and put her hands out, presumably to feel the heat, but Kev thought she wanted to take his hands so reached out then when Min lowered hers he laughed nervously.

"Oops, that was awkward," he giggled, brushing off the misunderstanding.

"My mistake," said Min.

"Guys, come in. It's freezing out there. Hurry up." Kev beckoned us in and zipped up behind us, the relief instant.

Anxious stirred, so I let him down and he trotted over to the open door of the van after sniffing Kev's leg and wagging that he was still a good guy.

"Thanks. Wow, it's so warm." I pulled my hat off and ran a gloved hand through my hair, not a smart move as now it was back to being freezing again.

"Take a seat. Enjoy the warmth. The diesel heater works amazingly well, and although it's a waste leaving the door open, it means I can cook with some space and not freeze. You hungry? Want a drink? Excuse me, but I've had a few. I'm trying to take it easy, but that's not working out so well." Kev indicated the bottle of Jack Daniels on the table, only a little gone, with mixers of cola beside it. "No need for a fridge, eh?" he chuckled.

"We're good, but thanks for the offer," I said. "You look like you're coping better than everyone else. The neighbour's awning collapsed last night, and our gazebo is a write-off. I'm going to invest in something stronger."

"Mate, it's part of the experience. The first year, I made every mistake there is to make, and had to replace a lot of my gear. Now I go for the absolute best. Trust me, it's worth the investment. Not cheap, but it works out better value in the long run as you don't need to keep replacing stuff. Get yourselves a diesel heater, is my advice. Perfect for these harsh winters."

"I think I will get one fitted once we get out of here," I said, having made up my mind. "Kev, are you okay here? We were worried, especially as you seemed down earlier, and you're on your own."

"I like being on my own. I'm great, thanks. Had my dinner, which was awesome. I did a chicken in the little table top oven I have, which is another thing worth investing in. Worked out fantastic. Now I'm going to relax and watch a movie. You two look like you've been busy though. I saw you coming and going a few times. Everyone else is keeping a low profile. I did spot the woman from the other van, and the guy is always popping in and out, but no kids. That's weird. Kids love the snow, right?"

"He's worried about the murder, which is understandable. And the children are happy in the motorhome playing, and listening to music. Did you speak to his wife?"

"Nope. Just saw her dashing around a few times, but I was in here. What's up? Anything else happened? I'm guessing it isn't solved. I spoke to the detective, and he seemed alright, and I told him about my past. He was cool. Mind you, I bet I'm the prime suspect." Kev laughed it off, but I could tell he hated that his past meant he would forever be looked at in a certain way when there was trouble nearby.

"Clarence is a good guy. He got attacked earlier, and we found him in the lane. He ended up in the village where, er, things got weird."

"Wow! Is he okay?"

"Fine. Nothing hurt but his pride. And a bump to the head, of course."

Kev wrung his hands and glanced at the bottle, and I noted that in the bin beneath the table there was an empty one. Maybe he'd already been on a bender and had slept off the worst? Or had he been out roaming and had attacked the DI? Not unless he had a spare Santa suit, and had then taken a different route back up here. I felt bad for even thinking it, but the truth was that everyone was a suspect.

"Yeah, I had a few earlier," admitted Kev as he caught me staring at the empty bottle. "But it wasn't full. Just a wee dram in the bottom. You must think I'm a right alcoholic."

"Kev, it's your business. You do what you want. We aren't judging."

"Liar!" he laughed, but he slumped into a chair and rubbed at his face. "Look, you both seem nice, and it's kind of you to check on me, but I just want to be left alone, you know."

"Sure. Sorry to intrude," said Min.

"I normally enjoy company, and trust me, usually I'm better at small talk, but I told you I had bad news and wanted to drown my sorrows, didn't I?"

"You did. We didn't want to pry."

"Thank you. Someone died. A friend. From back on the estate where I beat that guy up and ended up doing time. He never got out, and was caught up in a bad life. Now he's dead. It hit me hard, as I know it could have just as easily been me. Sorry, you don't want to hear this."

"You can talk to us if you want," I said.

"Nah, I'm good. I'm dealing with it in my own way. A few drinks, and time alone to clear my head and get my act together. You carry on looking into this, and if you need me, I'm here."

"Thanks, Kev. Look after yourself." I shook his hand and so did Min, then we roused Anxious and wrapped up before heading back out into the insane weather that threatened to destroy even Kev's awesome setup.

Battling the wind, snow, and now increasingly treacherous conditions, we made a beeline for the one remaining vehicle. How it had taken so long to make the visit felt like a true mystery, but events had conspired against us, and with absolutely no sign of them having been outside, it felt pretty safe to assume they hadn't been involved. Sure, they'd cleared the snow at some point in the night, the piles around the motorhome confirmed that, but there were no footsteps or signs of activity since then and so hopefully we could tick them off the list soon enough.

"Max, could Kev have done it? He's capable, and smart, and what if this is tied up with his friend dying? Maybe that man in the snowman killed his friend?"

"And what, he kidnapped the killer and brought him here to dole out his punishment?"

"Anything's possible. You never know. Or maybe he lost the plot last night and did it and can't even remember. Who knows?"

"He was acting a little off, sure, and he could have done it, but why? And who is the dead man?"

"That's the question everyone wants answered. Come on, let's see what these people have to say. Maybe they saw something and we can figure this out. Wouldn't that be great?"

"It sure would."

We approached, the going now nigh on impossible as the snow came over Min's knees and halfway up my shins. It got so bad that I had to give her a piggyback as otherwise she would have been rooted to the spot and turned into a Minsicle within minutes. As much as I fancied the idea of licking a static Min—and no, that isn't weird at all, I told myself as I smiled—it most likely wouldn't be great for her festive spirit.

The ride sure was though. We laughed our way to an appropriate distance from the large motorhome and got to inspect it close up for the first time. It was impressive, and huge, and no doubt had all the mod-cons. It was also a rental, so maybe this was just a couple, or group of friends, who fancied getting away for a few days but weren't into the vanlife scene thus hadn't ventured outside. It would have a fully-fitted kitchen, a bathroom, and a lovely sofa, too, so they were probably hunkered down and watching the TV after a sumptuous dinner.

Or, and I berated myself for not having thought of it earlier, they were murdered and the interior was a bloodbath.

"Um, Min, what if we've made a huge mistake, Clarence, too, and they're dead?"

"Gosh, I hadn't considered it. I assumed as there were no footprints that they were safe. Could the killer have snuck up from the rear through the woods?"

"Easily. Okay, maybe not easily, but it's possible. We better hurry just in case." I lowered her and she passed

Anxious to me as he was fretting and trying to get free, but he got worse when I held him.

"What's up, buddy? Are you scared? Cold?"

Anxious whined, eyes locked on the motorhome, and I got a sinking feeling in the pit of my stomach. Had we been lax and now the worst thing imaginable had happened?

Min reached out and stroked his head, but he ignored her. "He's acting really strange."

"What's got into him? Anxious, are you having a funny turn? Maybe it's the cold. He's got his jumper on, but it is freezing."

"Maybe we should put him back in Vee? Max, I'm getting worried. Look, he's trembling now."

Sure enough, Anxious was shaking uncontrollably and kept turning his head side to side as he snorted almost like he'd finally tracked a rabbit and this time he'd get it.

"Maybe we should take him home."

At the word, our usually well-behaved dog scratched at my arm manically, and as I moved it, he wriggled free, dropped into the snow with a dull thud, disappeared beneath it, then popped back up and pawed at the snow as he tried to get closer to the motorhome. With his face set in grim determination, I was surprised to see his tail whip up and circle happily, as though he was about to burst with excitement.

"Now he's acting like he's about to see his best friends. Which are us." I frowned as I watched the tiny dog struggle, but when I reached out to help him he shook me off, leapt high, then raced across the more compacted ground before sinking into a soft spot then popping up spitting snow and shaking his head.

"He wants to get to the people inside," said Min. "Maybe he knows they're in danger."

"He's not acting like they're in danger, but something's got into him for sure."

We hurried to catch up with the little guy, then I scooped him up and wrapped him in my arms tightly so he couldn't escape as I feared he'd hurt himself or freeze to death. We stomped over to the motorhome, grateful for the heavy duty awning that although laden with snow was still protecting the ground and left it if not free of snow then at least not quite as deep.

Anxious yipped loudly and whined, before somehow managing to wriggle free and once again he dropped down. This time, he was taking no chances, and scrambled forward on his belly, his legs dragging behind him like he was navigating an assault course, then he reached the steps, clambered up, and scratched at the door whilst barking insistently.

"Max, what is wrong with him?"

"I don't know. It's almost like..."

"What? Like what?" gasped Min, truly concerned now.

I couldn't help myself and burst out laughing. Suddenly, everything made sense. At least, Anxious' behaviour did. I was surprised it had taken him so long, actually, and was miffed I'd failed to pick up on the obvious signs.

"Min, don't you get it?" I asked above the din of his barking.

"Get what?"

"A rental motorhome that turned up late, the people inside have slept in, and are most likely still in bed. We had mystery presents and even a tree in the van, and now Anxious is super-excited and can't wait to get in there. Isn't it obvious?"

With a pout, Min said, "Max, I have absolutely no idea what you are talking about."

"It's—"

Suddenly, the door was flung open. Min jumped back, Anxious howled in delight, and I smiled as a vision in a white dress with festive red polka dots, wearing a matching bandanna and bright red high heels, her hair the usual red to match, beamed at us, her make-up flawless, her energy emanating like a lighthouse during a storm.

"Hello, Anxious," beamed Mum. "Hi, Max. Hi, Min. It's me, Mum. And er, I guess Min, you can call me Jill if you must, but I'd prefer Mum." Mum spread her arms wide and beckoned us forward for a hug, but Anxious got in there first and launched at her. Fearing for her dress, Mum sidestepped and Anxious went flying through the door and inside where I heard Dad shout out to shut the door as Mum was letting the cold in.

Before we had chance to do anything but gawp, Dad appeared, grumbling, "Close the door, you daft woman. It's freezing and you'll make my Irish coffee cold. Hurry up!" Dad glanced past Mum to us, then turned as Anxious pawed at his indigo Levi's 501s, the jeans he always wore as both he and Mum were fifties nuts and followed the fashion at all times. He bent and scooped up the excited dog, mindless of his pristine white T-shirt with the sleeves rolled up, his Brylcreemed black hair completing the Teddy Boy look he adored.

"Hey, Dad."

"Max! Min! At last. What took you so long?" Dad smiled warmly, but before we could answer, he added, "Get inside before my drink goes cold. Hurry up! Do you want one? How about a Baileys? I don't know why we only drink it at Christmas. I say to Jill every year that we should have it more often, then for some reason we forget until next year. Weird, eh?"

With an exchange of bemused smiles, Min and I hurried inside gratefully, only pausing for a hug from Mum which I knew would be impossible to avoid, not that I wanted to, and a hearty slap on the back from Dad.

Mum shut the door then turned to us and beamed. "Surprise!"

"It sure is," I laughed. "I can't believe I didn't figure out it was you guys. What are you doing here?"

"You don't mind, do you?" asked Dad. "We figured we'd surprise you. I know you invited us but we said no, which was your Mum's doing as she insisted we had to do a big Christmas with Ernie and his new wife and a load of distant relations nobody likes, but then she realised how awful that would be so we came here instead."

"I did not say they were awful. Loud, annoying, a headache, and they'd eat all our food and drink all our booze and we'd have to pay for everything, but I didn't say annoying."

"So, what have we missed? We got lost on the way so turned up late, then it snowed and we thought we were trapped, but we managed to clear around the motorhome so we could do your presents, but after that we were exhausted as it was early morning so we've only been up for an hour."

"And hitting the booze already, I see," I teased, noting the whisky bottle, the Baileys, and a few bottles of wine ready to go.

"It's Christmas," said Dad with a frown, as that explained all overindulgence at this time of year and nobody could give a good comeback to it.

"True," we both agreed.

"Um, so it was you who left the gifts?" asked Min. "You did the tree too?"

"Very funny! We saw that when we snuck in. It looked nice. What, thought it was Father Christmas who brought the presents, did you?" chuckled Dad, winking at me.

"No, of course not!" protested Min.

"No way!" I agreed.

"They did, Jill. They thought Santa had been. Silly sods. As if he'd get down the exhaust pipe. You need a chimney."

"Maybe I'll get a little wood burner for Vee," I mumbled.

"Good idea for next year," agreed Mum amiably, then bustled about dragging our hats off our heads without asking, unwinding our scarves, and tugging at the sleeves of our coats until we relinquished them.

"So, have you had a nice day so far?" asked Dad. "Did you open the presents? Were they okay?"

"We haven't actually had a chance yet. We were hoping to do them after we checked on the mad couple in the fancy motorhome."

"Oh, where are they? I didn't see another one as large as ours." Dad squinted out of the window, and we waited for the penny to drop, which it didn't.

"Are they a nice couple, Max?" asked Mum.

"I meant you guys, you utter crazies," I laughed.

"Hey, that's not nice," giggled Dad. He lifted his Irish coffee and said, "Cheers." Clearly, it wasn't his first.

"Cheers," we chorused, somehow finding we had a glass of something bubbly in our hands.

"Now, tell us everything," said Mum, lifting Anxious onto the counter so he could have a fuss before he exploded from cuddle withdrawal.

"It's a long story," I sighed, then sipped my wine.

Chapter 15

By the time we'd finished explaining everything, we'd demolished a bottle of wine, a pack of mince pies, a tub of Pringles, way too many chocolates, and Dad was deep into the Baileys while Mum was so far into it she was about to emerge the other side dripping with it. My parents were never ones to sit in silence while a tale was told, wanting to know every last detail and insisting on correcting us when they believed we'd said something wrong, which we clearly hadn't as we were the ones who'd experienced it.

"Looks like we've got our work cut out," said Dad. "See, Jill, I told you there would be a murder. How lucky are we?"

"Lucky?" I asked.

"Sure. Your mum reckoned no way there would be a murder on Christmas, but I told her, of course there would. It's an odd one, granted, but you two will figure it out." Anxious barked from Mum's arms, so Dad corrected himself. "You three," then winked at us.

"Dad, what happened? Why did you sneak into the van? And how?"

"We have a key," he mumbled.

"I never gave you a key."

Dad muttered under his breath so we couldn't quite catch it.

"What did you say? And shouldn't you have knocked? How do you have a key?"

"Your mother got one cut just in case."

"Of what?"

"Something awful," said Mum, coming to sit beside us on the comfortable sofa, the large table groaning under the weight of the Christmas treats.

"So you got a key cut without asking just in case you happened to be nearby and wanted to gain access?" I asked dubiously.

"Yes!" said Mum brightly.

"And you arrived late last night then snuck into Vee and put out presents, decorated a tree while we slept, then ate the mince pie, drank the milk, and munched on the carrot? You took Santa and Rudolph's snack?"

"Yes, that's right? said Dad merrily. "Hey, what? Wait a minute. We didn't steal any food or drink any milk. And we didn't bring a tree. Jill, did you eat the snacks?"

"Me? Of course not! You know I'm watching my weight."

Everyone studied the table full of Christmas treats I knew my folks adored. At this time of year, they always let themselves go and lamented their weight gain in the new year and joined the hordes of others who dieted for a month or two to recover.

"Yes, well, I might have indulged early," mumbled Mum.

"Guys, it's the afternoon and you haven't been up long. How have you eaten so much so quickly? Have you actually had your lunch?"

"We grazed," said Dad, popping a Celebrations chocolate into his mouth then almost choking when he realised he'd taken a Bounty. Why they put them in is anyone's guess; nobody likes coconut contaminating their guilty pleasures.

"So, what were you going to do about Christmas dinner?" I asked, already knowing the answer.

"We thought we'd have it with you," said Mum. "That's alright, isn't it?

"Of course, but if it wasn't for the murder we'd have already eaten. How come you slept so late?"

"Because we had to wrap the presents, take them to yours, shovel the snow away, and then we were wired because of the excitement so sat up having a cheeky tipple for a while."

"Yes," agreed Mum. "We got hammered and didn't wake up until gone one."

Dad shot her a glance which she ignored, and I couldn't help but laugh.

"Thank you both for coming," said Min diplomatically, although she cast a warning look my way. We both knew that my parents were a handful, and having them inside Vee with us would be a real squeeze to say the least. Already I was panicking about how it would work, not wanting to have to spend Christmas in this soulless, albeit large rental.

Winking, and nudging me in case I'd missed his very obvious gesture, Dad said, "Don't worry, Max, we have a plan."

"What kind of plan?" I asked warily, knowing that often their plans involved no work for them and a lot for me.

"We got you a present. Both of you, actually," said Mum, pushing Dad aside so she could sit, her outfit ensuring Dad had to slide off the seat to accommodate the very flared dress.

"That's nice," I stammered, my stomach flipping as they grinned at us.

"You bet it is. Wait here, I'll go and get it." Dad hurried off.

"Be careful!" shouted Mum.

"Of what?" he asked, popping his head out of the bedroom.

"Things," said Mum cryptically, eyes sparkling with excitement.

"What's this about, Mum?"

"You'll see."

"I thought the presents in Vee were from you?"

"They are. But this is your main present. They're just small things we knew you'd like, but this is something special. Love, sorry to spring our visit on you, and it's awful about the murder, but it is Christmas and we wanted to see you all. Anxious loves his grandma, and I knew he'd be pining for me."

"He does miss you," I admitted.

"Here it is!" Dad dragged a huge oblong of a present behind him as he navigated the narrow passage between the cupboards and kitchen then stood it on end.

"What on earth is that? It's five feet long. It's for us?"

"Sure is. Wanna unwrap it?"

"You fool, there's no room in here. They need to open it outside."

"But it's snowing out there," protested Dad.

"So? Our awning is giving us shelter, so they can do it there. Jack, you know they have to do it outside."

"Ah, yes, of course. Right you are then. Everyone get their gear on, we're going out. We haven't been outside since the early hours for your gifts, and the snow was coming down heavy by then. But thankfully, as we turned up so late to collect the motorhome, the nice man we rented it off supplied us with two snow shovels. We cleared around the van last night and now we can make some proper space out there. Max, how about me and you do that while the girls have a Baileys, then we can go out for the big reveal."

"What a great idea!" Mum clapped her hands, clearly relieved to avoid the manual labour.

I turned to Min and she nodded that it was fine, and although we were both rather taken aback by the whole turn of events, there was little choice as once my parents got an idea in their heads there would be no swaying them.

Dutifully, Dad and I wrapped up warm, he retrieved his wellies and the snow shovels, then we braced ourselves as he flung the door open, expecting the worst.

"The snow's stopped and the winds gone," I told the others. "And the sun's out. Wow! It's lovely out there. The sun's really bright and everything's sparkling."

"See you soon." Min blew me a kiss, and not to be outdone, Mum blew one for me then one for Dad. She glared at us, so we hastily pretend caught the kisses and slapped them to our cheeks. She nodded her satisfaction before ignoring us and focusing on pouring two very generous servings of the infamous creamy liqueur.

We got straight to work, the physical activity welcome. It was just what I needed to put everything into perspective, meaning I didn't think about it and merely focused on shovelling snow and enjoying spending time with my father. Times like this were always golden, and we settled into an easy silence interspersed with grunts and the sound of the snow shovels scraping through the ice.

Dad was as strong as an ox, and gave me a good run for my money as we worked hard, neither of us wanting to rest first, the sweat building, the ache in my arms enjoyable as we gave the task our all, enjoying the simple pleasure of working hard. We grinned as we battled the weather and got stuck in, and in no time we'd cleared the snow from under the canopy, exposing glorious green grass I hadn't realised I'd missed so much until I saw it.

"Good job," said Dad with a slap on my back.

"You too. But why are we clearing it so thoroughly? What's the deal?"

Dad frowned, then scratched at his head before removing his hat and sorting out his hair. "Um, you better ask your mother."

"What are you two up to?"

"Nothing. Why would we be up to something?"

"Because you always are."

Dad laughed heartily, something I always loved about him and Mum. They were so positive, and it had rubbed off on me; I always tried to follow their lead and look on the positive side of life.

"Let's get the girls out and we can show you your gift."

"Dad, do you swear you didn't eat Santa's food? If so, who did?"

"Son, it wasn't us. You heard your mother. I remember seeing it in the van, and would never touch it. I guess it was the big man."

"Santa?" I laughed.

"Who else?"

"You're kidding, right?" I couldn't tell if he was serious or not, but his body language screamed that he was telling the truth.

"There are a few things in this life that I never joke about, and a visit from Father Christmas is one of them. It wasn't us, so it must have been him."

"But you don't believe…"

"What? Don't believe what?"

"Nothing, it doesn't matter." This was getting weird, even for me, and living with the two fifties nuts meant I knew weird better than most.

"Right you are!" With a smile, Dad rapped on the door and called for Min and Mum to come out.

We waited longer than either of us had hoped, but not as long as we expected, as Mum was not a woman to do things by half measures, and took extreme pride in her appearance at all times. She had never once come out of her bedroom in all the years of me growing up without her hair done, fully dressed for the day, with her make-up immaculate.

By the time the door opened, our sweat had dried, leaving us colder than ever and shivering. Anxious bolted for freedom, eyes wide in shock and delight when he spied the cleared ground, and ran a lap then cocked a leg, grinning and sighing as he relieved himself.

"Well, I guess he missed the grass too," laughed Dad.

"Guess so."

Min jumped down and joined us, almost as excited as Anxious to see the grass. With a hug for us both, we spun to find Mum standing in the doorway, a deep frown on her face. Dressed in a red woollen hat with a white pom-pom to match her dress, and a red duffle coat, she looked like Santa's wife, but she wasn't happy.

Our eyes tracked down, following Mum's, until all attention focused on her bright red, shiny Wellington boots.

"You okay, love?" asked Dad nervously. He sidestepped behind me, then called out, "You look lovely."

"I do not! These stupid things hide my calves, and you know I like to show off my lower legs. They feel horrendous. So clunky and heavy, and how are you supposed to walk properly? They're so flat."

"Mum, they're wellies. They're meant to be flat so you can grip the slippery ground. And they hide your calves so you don't get wet legs. They look nice. Very nice. Right, everyone?"

"Smashing," said Dad, hands on my shoulders, peeking out then ducking back for fear her glare would melt first him then the snow in a five-mile radius.

"You got a lovely colour," said Min, stifling a giggle.

"Thank you, dear. And Jack, what are you doing back there? Are you tired?"

"Eh? No, not me," he laughed nervously. "You coming down, love?"

"I told you, I can't walk in these things. I feel like I've shrunk. I need the height of my heels. I feel underdressed."

"The last thing anyone would say about your attire is that you look underdressed." I winked at Min who was fit to bursting, but when Mum grumbled then cast her steely gaze at us, her mirth soon vanished.

"Stupid things. I like to look my best in case we have visitors, and how can I do that wearing these awful things?"

"It's winter, love. And wet and cold and there's lots of snow. You'll be fine."

"Doubt it." Nevertheless, Mum carefully took the steps down then stood on the grass, wobbling from side to side as she tried to get accustomed to the alien footwear. "It feels weird. Like I'm sinking into the ground. Am I shrinking?" she yelped, reaching out and grabbing Min then hanging on for dear life, like the ground was swallowing her.

"Mum, you aren't shrinking. You're just exceptionally short." I knew immediately that the joke was in bad taste, at least for her, as not even Min cracked a smile, most likely because Mum had her talons deep into her shoulders and she was wincing in pain.

Dad gripped my own shoulders tighter, ducking back behind me, and whispered, "You're for it now."

Mum spun slowly, like something from a horror movie where a doll turns its head, and fixed her made-up eyes on me, boring through my skull, into my brain, then began the process of melting the cells through force of will alone. When I felt the ooze coming out of my ears, I held my hands up and said, "I'm sorry. I was only joking. You're the perfect height."

"Of course I am. I'm nearly as tall as Min. Um, when I wear my heels."

"Min's only five five," shouted Dad, then ducked back behind me.

"Coward," I hissed.

"Exactly," crowed Mum. "Perfect." Mum stomped about, releasing Min, who gasped as she rubbed at her shoulder, while we grouped together by the door, finally releasing our shovels as it seemed like we'd live to make fun of Mum another day.

"Well, what are you waiting for, Jack? Get the gift."

"Right you are," he said, relieved, then hurried inside before emerging with the huge parcel.

He laid it on the ground, then we stood around in a circle, and things became awkward when nobody said a word.

Finally, exasperated, I asked, "Should we open it?"

"Of course." Mum beamed, Dad grinned, so with a shrug, Min and I stepped forward and pulled off the soggy paper, revealing...

"A gazebo!? How did you know we'd need another one?"

"Because you didn't get the absolute best before. You should have done your homework, like me," crowed Dad.

"This one has a better pitch on the roof thing, has thicker guide ropes, and—"

"They're guy ropes, love," corrected Dad.

"Don't be daft. Why would they be called guy ropes? They're guide ropes, to guide people to walk around them. So silly." Mum patted the top of Dad's head and smiled in sympathy at the perceived mistake. Min and I didn't correct her, neither did Dad.

"It looks great," I said, checking out the label on the large bag containing the gazebo.

"It should. Cost a fortune. It's reinforced, and what all seasoned travellers use. It's got better stitching, is guaranteed waterproof for five years, and has super lightweight but sturdy poles. You can open it up or use the screens, and it has insect mesh too. Plus, there are loads of pockets for your doodahs, and it's guaranteed not to collapse even under heavy snow loads. Merry Christmas, Son. Merry Christmas, Daughter."

"Merry Christmas to you both."

"Thanks so much. This is genuinely a great gift. I'm so sorry, but we didn't get you anything. We don't normally do presents."

"That's okay. We weren't expecting anything," said Mum.

We turned to Min, who was yet to speak, and I was shocked to find she was crying.

"What's the matter? It's nice, isn't it?" I asked, concerned. Anxious whined from her feet so she picked him up and stroked him, letting the tears flow.

Min shifted her attention from Anxious, who was busy licking her cheeks to lap up the salty tears, and focused not on me but on Dad. "You called me Daughter."

"Well, yes, of course," he said, nonplussed.

"Is that how you feel?"

"About what?"

"About me?"

"I'm not following, love?" Dad turned to Mum for a little help.

"She's feeling emotional. It's because it's Christmas. And the murder," Mum explained.

"No, it isn't that. It's just, I… I miss you guys. All of you. All of it. Being a proper family. You called me Daughter. Am I?"

"Not by blood, no," said Dad, as blunt as always. "But we've always thought of you as our daughter. Of course we have. And you still are, no matter what our idiot son did to ruin things. Whatever happens between you two, you'll always be family."

"Of course she will," tutted Mum. "Min, you know that, don't you? You're our family. And we just know that everything will work out fine in the end. You two were made for each other. Two peas in a pod. The perfect couple."

"Thank you so much!" Still clutching Anxious, she dashed to them and wrapped her arms around my accommodating parents. I couldn't have been more proud of them.

Drying her eyes with a rather startled dog, Min came back to herself, smiled at Anxious, let him down, then came to me and said, "Max, you have the best parents ever."

"I know."

"Right, let's get this over to your van and clear the snow there so we can put this up. I imagine Max is getting jittery without his kitchen, and there's no way he can cook a proper feast inside Vee. It's too small. We need some space so we can sit out and have drinks and a real nosh-up." Dad grabbed the gazebo, pointed at the shovels, so Min and I retrieved them, then we traipsed over to Vee, Mum complaining the whole time about shrinking and how on earth did people walk in flats rather than heels as it felt anatomically wrong, and that her feet hurt.

Once again, Dad and I got to work, and with a lot of effort managed to clear the snow from around Vee and sort out the kitchen area, which lifted our spirits. Vee was a sight to behold, like she'd had a good jet wash, shining in the sunshine as though she was just off the factory floor.

We then set to work assembling the new gazebo, and I had to admit it was impressive. Sturdy, very well made, more spacious, and surprisingly warm given how cold it was. The thick yet breathable material trapped the heat well, but still afforded plenty of ventilation for the warm months, and I just knew this was the final piece of the puzzle to continue my vanlife adventures in comfort and style. Even the white and orange colour scheme matched Vee, which showed how much thought my parents had put into choosing this.

Ten minutes after erecting it, the chairs were placed, the table and outdoor kitchen set up how I liked it, and dinner had been moved to the much larger double hob so I could keep an eye on it while we sipped our drinks and enjoyed a few nibbles.

Life was just about perfect.

Apart from the corpse up at the house.

Chapter 16

With the gazebo erected as close as possible to Vee as I wouldn't be moving the van anyway, we left the one side completely open to afford easy access. It was a revelation. After always erecting the shelter a short distance away for ease of driving back and forth, having it close meant the living space was quadrupled. With the opposite screen lowered enough to afford a view, but with the insect mesh left in place, the wind was diffused but it didn't feel like we were trapped inside.

"This is perfect," sighed Dad, hunkered down with his coat up around his neck and his hat pulled low.

"Thank's so much, guys. This was a truly great present. I can't believe how different it is to the old one. I thought I'd got the best, but it doesn't compare to this."

"You've got your dad to thank for that. He spent days searching online, going through vanlife forums, and even joining a few camping ones so he could ask questions."

"It was nothing." Dad waved it away, looking bashful, which wasn't like him at all.

"You worked hard at it," said Mum, confused by his reticence.

"Thanks, Dad. You chose well. I appreciate the work you put in. It's awesome."

"Good choice, Jack," said Min.

"Now, how about you open the other presents?" suggested Mum, rubbing her hands together.

"Can we?" Min was up in a flash and already inside rummaging around. "I love Christmas," she called out in a high-pitched squeal.

Anxious leapt up and ran inside to see what was so exciting, then they both emerged, Min with an armful of gifts, Anxious with one between his teeth.

"I see the little fella found his," giggled Mum, her smile beautiful. She always loved watching people unwrap gifts.

"I'm amazed he waited this long," said Min.

"Make sure everyone gets the right one," ordered Mum. She explained what was what, then we crowded around the blanket as Min and I opened the various presents. By the time we had only one left each, we both had plenty of socks for the year, enough Marks and Spencer underwear to last at least a decade, sufficient chocolate to survive a zombie apocalypse, and a large bottle of Baileys each, which we vowed to sample through the year and not just forget about and leave in the back of a cupboard until next Christmas.

"Thanks so much," I said, kissing Mum and hugging Dad.

"Yes, thank you so much. We feel bad for not getting you anything. We didn't even buy each other a present as we promised not to, but this was so kind."

"It was nothing. Just a few little things for you both." Mum leaned forward, eyes dancing with excitement, as she ordered, "Now, open the last one each. We saved the best to last."

"We sure did," laughed Dad, eyes lingering on Mum, full of love and adoration as always.

"More socks?" I teased.

"Nope." Mum crossed her arms and beamed at Dad, both very smug.

"I'm intrigued," I admitted, knowing that as a grown man I shouldn't be quite as excited, but no matter your age, there's something magical about opening presents. I truly did feel bad about not having bought them anything, but for years now all four of us had agreed not to exchange gifts and rather to spend it on nice food we'd never otherwise buy.

"Max, you go first." Min's eye twitched as she eyed her one remaining gift greedily, her fingers flexing.

I laughed and said, "No, it's fine. You open yours first."

"Oh, thanks. I can't wait!" With eager hands, Min just about resisted the urge to tear the paper off and instead took her time, peeling away the tape carefully, trying like she always had to unwrap the gift without ripping the wrapping paper so it could be re-used.

Confronted with a plain cardboard box, Mix cast a quizzical eye to Mum and Dad who both pretend zipped their mouths shut, everyone now leaning forward to await the grand reveal. Beyond excited, and with Anxious sniffing at the box as his gift, a large chewy, had been opened and devoured without any thought about the paper, Min opened the box then tipped out the contents.

"No way!" she gasped, glancing up at my folks who were beaming.

"Do you like it?" asked Dad.

"I chose it," said Mum, keen to get the praise.

"Thank you so much. It's wonderful." Carefully, Min picked up the surprise present to inspect it properly, turning it over and over in her hands before glancing at me and smiling. "Think I'm worthy?"

"Of course you are," I chuckled, eyeing the gift jealously. "But does this mean...?"

"Maybe it does, maybe it doesn't," she teased, cheeks flushed with gratitude. Min stood and kissed Mum and Dad, both as proud as I'd ever seen them. "Thank you so much. It truly means a lot."

Anxious cocked his head, trying to understand what the fuss was about, so Min bent and he scooted over then sniffed the gift.

"He doesn't know what it is," laughed Dad.

Min waved the piece of paper in front of Anxious and explained. "It's a railcard, Anxious. It lets me get on a train anywhere in the country, any time I want, for a whole six months. No booking, no paying crazy prices, and no umming and ahing about if I should come and visit you and Max or not. This must have cost a fortune." She gnawed her lip as she raised her eyes to my merry parents.

"Not as much as you'd think. And let's be honest, we have an ulterior motive," said Mum.

"That's right. This way, you can always visit Max wherever he might be without stressing about travel so much. And if you want an adventure of your own, you can have one."

"That was very kind of you both," I said.

"Now open yours," suggested Dad.

Keen to discover what they'd got me, I unwrapped mine, making a mess of the paper no matter how hard I tried to be careful, then studied the box matching Min's. Inside, I found a slip of paper, and cast my eyes to the smiling faces. "Another railcard?" I teased, knowing it wouldn't be.

"Read it," said Dad.

"A gym membership! Guys, this is great. I've been meaning to get one for ages, but how did you know?"

"Because your father has been reading vanlife forums and Facebook groups, and they all agree on one thing. You need a gym membership so you can use the facilities. Saunas, jacuzzis, have a workout, too, if you want, but it's the luxury showers this chain are best known for. Plus, swimming pools, and they even have dog care facilities at some of the large ones. How cool is that?"

"Very. You're right, showering at campsites isn't the best, although I'm used to it, but a gym membership will make all the difference. This chain has places everywhere, and you can bet I'll be using it every week."

Mum and Dad were beyond pleased with our reactions, and they truly were exceptional and expensive gifts, and exactly what we both wanted but would never have bought for ourselves. Their insight and thoughtfulness was unusual as they were often oblivious to things, but this time they'd really thought about it and I gave them both a massive hug, apologising again for not having bought them anything.

"We have all we want, and then some," said Dad. "And it's us who broke the agreement not to buy anything. We just wanted to show you both how much we love you."

"You soppy old sod," teased Mum, kissing Dad's cheek which made him beam with happiness.

"Hello? Anyone in there?" called DI Clarence Carroll.

"It's the killer!" shrieked Mum, jumping up and shoving at Dad so he toppled over backwards in his chair and landed with his legs up in the air.

"You maniac!" he moaned, rolling sideways then springing to his feet.

"Oops," giggled Mum, seemingly over her shock and now clutching her own chair as if she could fend off a horde of homicidal maniacs.

"Clarence, come in," I sighed, shaking my head at the two fools.

"Why did you push me over?" grumbled Dad.

"So you could protect me from the madman. Sorry, love, I got scared."

"It's the detective," I explained, unzipping the wall and beckoning Clarence inside.

With a nod, then a frown when he realised we had company and with wrapping paper all over the rug, he stepped back, ready to leave. "Sorry to disturb you. I didn't know you had guests." With a raised eyebrow, he took in the scene with an expert eye then nodded, clearly happy that we weren't in any trouble.

"Clarence, this is my mum, Jill, and dad, Jack."

"Jack and Jill? Max and Min?" he asked, just like so many others had in the past.

"That's right, love," said Mum merrily, resuming her seat. "What of it?"

"It's just that your names are, er, very nice!" he declared, realising Mum and Dad were oblivious to the obvious nursery rhyme or that mine and Min's names were rather comical.

They never had got it, and I doubted they ever would. Sometimes I wondered if they were pretending to be so vacant about certain things, then remembered that this was how they'd always been and part of their charm, even if it had caused frustration and embarrassment over the years.

"Guys, this is the detective I told you about. He's running the case single-handed and has been out in the freezing weather since this morning. Clarence, take a seat and let me make you a drink."

"Thanks, that would be great. It's so cold now, and the wind's nasty. Wow, it's surprisingly warm in here. How did you get a new gazebo today of all days?"

"We bought it," said Mum, chest swelling with pride.

Dad nodded and said, "Anything for our Max and Min."

"That's very generous." Clarence sank into the chair gratefully and sighed. "My feet are killing me. It's like I've done a marathon. It's so hard wading through snow, and it came down really heavy just before I left the pub. Bunch of crazies in there." Clarence removed his hat and rubbed at his head, the skin pink from exertion, but he was clearly frozen to the bone.

"Let me adjust the heater so it's pointing at you," I offered, then arranged it in Vee and the blast of warm air made us gasp with pleasure.

"That is so good. Awesome gazebo." Clarence turned to my folks and asked, "I assume you're in the large motorhome? I tried to speak to you earlier, but there was no answer. I did knock. Repeatedly."

"Sorry, but we were up late and slept in. Seems like we missed all the fun," said Dad.

With a staccato laugh, he said, "You sure did. Your son seems to have a knack for getting caught up in murder mysteries, and has been a great help."

"I wrote his wiki page!" blurted Dad.

"And it's very informative."

"How did it go at the pub?" asked Min.

"A nightmare," he sighed. "Everyone wanted to gossip, they all had an opinion on who the killer was, although nobody had proof or even a reason beyond old arguments or neighbours they disliked because they always left their wheelie bins out too long after collection day. The usual small village nonsense. Them all being dressed as Santa didn't help, and the amount of beer they'd consumed certainly made my job harder. What a day."

"You must be starving," said Mum with sympathy. "Have you eaten? And how about a drink? We have Baileys, and wine, and what else, Max?"

"I think Clarence is trying to steer clear of the booze, Mum," I explained, raising my eyebrows at him to check.

"A Baileys would be good. But don't worry, Max, I'm not about to go at it hard. I am on duty and will remain so until I catch my killer."

"Our Max is the one who solves the crimes," tutted Mum.

"Mum, he's a detective. And a very helpful one. This time, it's doubtful it will be me who solves it."

Mum and Dad giggled and shook their heads at me like I was foolish, and Dad explained, "Max, you always solve it. I'm sure the detective is a very capable man, but you see things nobody else does, pick up on the little details even the best detectives overlook, so no offence, Clarence, but you can chill and have a few drinks if you want. Max will solve it."

"Your faith is commendable," said Clarence, taking a drink with a grateful nod, then adding, "but please bear in mind that we have a very serious situation here. The weather is making everything extremely difficult, nobody seems to know anything, and the way the poor man was killed and left like that means there is a very real chance of harm coming to anyone involved. My advice is to lock up, never go anywhere alone, and yes, that includes the bathroom, and whatever you do, don't go delving too deeply into this. We don't know who's responsible, which means anyone could have done it. Don't get pally with people, don't take a stranger up on an invite into their home," Min and I exchanged a guilty glance at his words, as despite us knowing better we'd done exactly that with the elderly couple, "and please, whatever you do, do not confront anyone you suspect without me there. Are we clear?"

"He's such a spoilsport," complained Mum, topping up Clarence's drink without him asking.

"That's enough, thanks," he said, eyeing the glass greedily.

"So, who's the number one suspect?" asked Dad.

"That's where it gets tricky. The owners seem suspicious, but that might just be me reading too much into their actions. Something isn't right there, but I can't put my finger on it."

"You felt it too?" asked Min.

"I did. The way they've gone about things today seems weird. Why clear the track but not the campsite? People might want to leave. Who wouldn't after what's happened? But nobody can get out. Granted, there's nowhere to go as all the main routes are impassable, but it's still odd."

"Did they explain why?" I asked.

"Said it was so people could get up here and they could ferry people down if they wanted, but I'm not so sure."

"That makes sense, though, right?" asked Dad.

"Sure, but something's niggling at me. Maybe they just panicked and wanted to do something, but they seem level-headed otherwise. Sorry, I shouldn't be discussing this with you, but with no other officers, I needed to vent."

"What about everyone else? Have you spoken to them all now?"

"Mostly. The couple are nice. I had a long chat with Kev in the smart Transit, and checked his history. He admitted to having served time, but I don't judge people, and from what I can tell he's just doing his best to cope with a sad situation after a friend died."

"And what about Sam and the family?" I asked. "He seems friendly, but we haven't seen the others."

"I spoke to him, but apparently there are children and a baby so his wife hasn't stepped foot outside apart from when we saw her earlier. She was with the baby when I checked on them, but I can't see that they're going to be off on the rampage with a van full like that."

"Who does that leave us with? You saw your attacker head to the village, so what about the locals?"

"It could be anyone," Clarence sighed, swirling his drink then taking a sip and letting his shoulders relax. "Ah, that's so good. I needed it. Now, much as I hate to say it, but I have to go. There are things to check and I need time to think, so I'm going to wander around and see if I can uncover anything."

"Like what?" asked Min.

"Who knows?" he laughed. "This is the reality of police work. You do a lot of walking, plenty of mundane stuff, and speak to people who would rather talk to anyone but the law. It is what it is."

"I'll come out with you," I offered. "Stretch my legs."

"We'll wait here, Son," said Dad, looking comfortable and content with his drink.

"I'll stay too," said Min.

"See you all soon."

Clarence and I stepped outside into the sunshine, the cold at odds with the clear sky, but at least the wind had died down. We moved to the tree line then made a circuit looking for anything out of the ordinary, but the ground was pristine, the snow deep, impassible in places because of drifts against the fence, and we made it back to where we started without uncovering anything of interest.

At a loss, I suggested we check out the scene of the snowman again, partly because the snow there was the most compacted so we could stand without sinking, but also because it was where we'd found the notebook earlier and it was where Sam's wife had passed by.

"This is becoming a little too common," Clarence sighed as we approached and spotted what was clearly a leather wallet right where the snowman had been.

"And no way did we overlook that earlier. What is going on here?"

"I have no idea. But I intend to find out." Clarence pulled off his warm gloves, slipped on blue disposable ones, then photographed the scene before placing a marker and retrieving the wallet. He flipped it open, then turned to me and said, "At least we know who we're looking for now, and it's not what I expected."

Curious, I looked over his shoulder, shocked by the information I read.

Chapter 17

"That can't be right, surely?"

Clarence's resigned look seemed to indicate he wasn't convinced, but nevertheless he rifled through the wallet, pulling out every bank card, note, an old business card, even the man's national insurance card and one indicating he would like to be an organ donor after death. There wasn't much chance of that happening now, but it was nice to know he'd considered such things. I made a mental note to sign up myself, and also to go and donate blood at the next opportunity. I hadn't done it for years.

"It most definitely is right. There's no denying his ID. His driver's license confirms this is one Mitchell Jones."

"And his business card says he's a landscape gardener. If that's the case, how come Maddie and Roy reckon they've never seen the guy before? I assume he must have been from the village and works up here. They said themselves they had quite a lot of work done to the grounds, so what gives?"

"That's exactly what I'd like to know. His home address is from the next village over, which I assume is why none of the locals know of anyone missing, but it's still strange nobody has reported him going AWOL, especially today. Shame we don't have his phone, but it wouldn't surprise me if someone lets us find that next."

"Clarence, why is someone leaving things like this for us to find? I don't get it?"

"Me either. It's beyond weird. Whoever is doing it certainly knows more than they're willing to share in person, unless it's the killer himself who is leaving these pieces of evidence."

"They aren't going to do that. But then the question is, how did they get their hands on the book and wallet? And why would the killer have left them somewhere easy to find?"

"Unless they thought they'd hidden them well, of course." Clarence took another few minutes to go through everything again, and even called the number on the business card, but, as expected, there was no answer.

"What now?"

"Now I'm going to contact the station, speak to my boss at home, and between us we should be able to get someone out to his address. I know a few guys who live in the village, and although it might be impossible to drive there, they can go and knock on the door. Sure, they'll be annoyed, but not nearly as annoyed as I am right now. Max, someone's playing with us, and I for one do not like it one bit. Time to get answers." Clarence wandered off, eyes on his phone, then made a few calls before returning. My feet were numb and my back ached, but there was no way I could leave before I knew what on earth was happening.

Was it Sam's wife who had left the notebook earlier? And why hadn't Clarence insisted on talking to her? Maybe now he would.

"Any luck?" I asked when he returned.

"Yes, and it shouldn't take long. I spoke to a young officer who lives a few streets away, so he's going around there right now. Give it ten minutes and we might have ourselves some answers. In the meantime, we're going to chat with Sam and his wife. I want to hear from her why she was so close to where we found the notebook.

We battled the snow, which was becoming beyond tiresome, then rapped on the door and waited. Inside, everyone sounded like they were in high spirits as usual, and in the middle of a game by the sounds of it.

Sam answered the door looking flushed and excited, but that might have just been Christmas cheer as he certainly looked and smelled like he'd been indulging.

"Hi." Sam raised an inquisitive eyebrow and asked, "Is there a problem? Do you have news? Please tell me you've caught the killer."

"I'm afraid not. We'd like to speak to your wife, please. Is that okay?"

"Um, not really. She's over at the facilities taking a shower. I told her she was crazy, but she has this thing where she does cold showers every day. It's supposed to help you lose weight, so I guess today of all days is a good day to do it." Sam chuckled as he shook his head, clearly thinking it was as crazy as us.

"Thank you, Sir. We'll head over there now."

"Um, okay. Anything else?"

I was aware of how quiet it had become, the children having paused the game, and I began to feel bad for intruding, especially today. They must be upset, and Sam was doing a great job of trying to make it a fun Christmas for them.

"That's all. Sorry to keep being a nuisance," said Clarence. "I know this is meant to be a fun and exciting day. Are the children alright?"

"Fine. Coping very well in fact. If you don't mind, I'd rather you didn't speak to them. I've downplayed the whole thing and just want to get out of here as soon as possible."

"I understand completely. Of course I will respect your wishes. We'll go over to the showers now to have a quick chat with your wife. Nothing to worry about. Just routine."

"Of course. Just let her get dressed first," laughed Sam.

With a curt nod, Clarence spun on his heels and headed towards the modern shower block. I smiled at Sam, then hurried to catch him up.

Halfway there, he made a sharp turn and headed towards Kev's smart Transit.

"Why are you going there?" I asked.

"Call it a hunch. It's too much of a coincidence that we found the wallet, Max, and I want to check on Kev just to be sure."

I said nothing and followed in his wake, grateful for the easier going in his footsteps. At the tent, the DI called out hello then opened the zip, catching Kev unawares. He was just taking off his coat and removing his wellies, and slipping on a pair of envy-inducing orange Crocs—even I wasn't that brave. You'd see them a mile off.

"Been somewhere?" Clarence didn't wait for an invite, which I found out of character and surely must break rules of conduct for a serving officer. It may not have been a house as such, but surely the same rules applied and the police couldn't just enter without permission?

"Eh? Yeah, went to the loo. Why? And you shouldn't barge in like that. This is my home."

"Ah, my mistake. I forgot." Clarence knew exactly what he was doing, I was sure of that, but I remained quiet.

"Sir, I would like you to explain exactly what you just did. Bear in mind, we were outside and can trace your footsteps. You were over where the body was discovered this morning, were you not?"

"Look, what is this? So what if I was? I wanted to take a look. Offer my condolences to the poor guy, whoever he was. That's no way to go out." Kev slipped on his other Croc then arranged his boots by the entrance. Blowing into his hands, he opened the door to the van and the heat blasted us. I could have stayed there for the rest of the day.

"Very kind of you. Did you happen to take a walk into the village earlier? Possibly have a beer or two?"

Kev bristled, and I caught the slightest shift of his eyes back towards the van. Without making it obvious, I glanced through the door and saw what looked like a Santa costume on the counter opposite. Kev took a small step to his right, blocking the view, then scowled at the DI. "So what if I did?

There's no law against that. Why are you picking on me? I had a few beers to cheer myself up. You know this is a bad time for me and I can have some drinks if I want. I'm not doing anyone any harm."

"Nobody said you were. Sorry to intrude. That will be all. Enjoy the rest of your day, but please stay inside if you possibly can. It's dangerous out here with the killer on the loose." Clarence's phone rang so he waved to Kev then stepped outside, leaving us alone.

"What's with that guy? He was friendly earlier, but now he's acting like I'm the number one suspect."

"He's just stressed and tired. Sorry he was so harsh with you. Think nothing of it. Look, I know it's none of my business, but what's with the Santa costume?"

Kev frowned, clearly annoyed at my suspicious question. "Mate, I know the DI got attacked by someone in a Santa costume, but that's not cool you thinking I did it."

"I had to ask. Sorry."

"If you must know, I'm dropping in on some friends tomorrow. They have kids, and I always dress up. It's a yearly thing we do. They know it's me, and to be fair they're a little old for it, but it's just in good fun. That satisfy you?"

"Yes, and sorry again. I like you, Kev, so please forgive me."

"Sure. Whatever."

I smiled, then left, feeling bad but also not dismissing him as a suspect. Like everyone else here, something felt off about him. He seemed like a genuinely nice guy, and was forthcoming about his past when he didn't have to be, but I still had my reservations. Was I becoming jaded after so many murders? Losing my faith in humanity? I hoped not, but couldn't help wondering.

I zipped up the entrance, and heard Kev pop open a bottle, then turned to see Clarence jabbing at his phone then pocketing it, frowning and clearly not happy.

"Bad news?"

"Not so much bad as not helpful. That was the local copper from Mitchell's village. He couldn't gain entry and nobody answered, so he went around and spoke to the neighbours on either side. They weren't too impressed to be dragged from the TV and their families, but they gave him the lowdown on our victim. He was single, kept to himself, worked hard, and often came back very late, but was always friendly and very polite."

"And he was a landscape gardener?"

"Yes. And apparently a good one. Always had plenty of work. Did building and carpentry too. A Jack of all trades."

"So, what's the issue?"

"According to his neighbours, he hasn't been seen for a couple of days. They assumed he was visiting family, although they didn't know where or who and he'd never had any family visit him. Seems like the neighbours were the busybody types so knew everyone's business, and Mitchell was your typical loner. Never had any visitors, no friends they knew of, but was happy enough and always helpful to the elderly couple on the one side. The only weird thing is that his truck isn't there and that's why they believed he was away. Unless we happen to find it like we have our other clues, then it's a true mystery where it is. If he didn't drive, how did he get here, and how long has he been up here? I'm no expert, but to me it looks like he was killed last night. Where was he in the meantime?"

"That's really interesting. What are you thinking?"

"That we need to have another chat with the owners. Max, I'm sorry you had to see that with Kev, but I wanted to be sure about him. Did you see the Santa costume?"

"I did. I asked him."

"You have a sharp eye. I guess the stories about you are true, eh? What did he say?"

"That he's visiting friends tomorrow and always dresses up."

"Makes sense. I think he's a decent fella, but don't rule him out. I need a drink. Do you mind? Won't report me or anything?" Clarence waved his flask at me and I shook my head, then he took a generous swig, not looking like it was helping as guilt was written large on his face.

"It's a real problem for you, isn't it?"

"You don't know the half of it. I'm trying, Max, and have been doing pretty well. Yes, I got wasted last night, but I've been handling it well for almost a year now. Today's just a bad day to be dealing with a murder. You get me? I'm on my own, no family like it used to be, and it's hard."

"I understand. And of course I won't tell anyone. You do what you feel is best."

"That's just the thing. I know it isn't the best thing for me, but I do it anyway." Chuckling, and shaking his head, he took another snifter than stowed the flask.

"Clarence?"

"Hmm?"

"You said we should talk to the owners. You want me with you?"

"Oh, sorry, I shouldn't have said that. Max, you get back to your family and that incredible ex-wife of yours. Mate, you seem so in love. I can't believe you're divorced."

"I messed up big time and she divorced me. I obsessed over work as a chef and neglected what was most important. It took the breakup for me to get my act together. I quit work, sorted my affairs, sold the house I'd bought after we split up, and now I can live off other property investments I have and live this life. It's been good for us both. Next year we should be back together, but there are no guarantees and I keep expecting her to realise I'm not good enough for her."

"Don't sell yourself short. You're a great guy, and not many would go to such lengths to fight for the woman they love, so you should be proud. I wish I could do the same, but it's too late for me."

"Want to talk about it?"

Clarence laughed, and shook his head, patting his pocket but refraining from taking another drink. "You absolutely do not want to hear about it. I'm a walking train wreck. It's over for me and the missus, but you should fight for your wife with every ounce of your being."

"I intend to. Now let's go and talk to the owners before I have to prepare dinner."

We walked in silence, and I took a moment to enjoy the clear sky and the shining sun that was fast sinking. Before we even got to the house it had vanished behind the trees, plunging everything into a twilight that sent the temperature plummeting instantly and both of us shivering as we hurried to our destination.

Maddie and Roy were outside the static home arguing as we approached. Maddie was gesticulating at the house, Roy was shaking his head and raging, fists clenched, and we sped up for fear it would turn nasty.

By the time we arrived things had calmed down, and rather than fisticuffs, the couple were hugging.

"Everything alright here?" asked Clarence.

"Fine," said Maddie with a frown of confusion.

"We were just having a slight disagreement," explained Roy.

"Care to share?"

"Not really, no. It's private."

"Roy, just tell him. We don't want him to suspect us."

"And why would I?" asked Clarence.

"Come on. Don't treat us like fools. We know we're suspects. Why wouldn't we be? We own the place, should have heard it happen, and we're strapped for cash and now we get a murder. Of course you suspect us." Roy stomped his feet, clearly having been outside for a while, his cheeks rosy and the ground around the house and cabin well trampled.

"Fair enough," laughed the DI. "So, what's the problem?"

"Roy wants me to clear the campsite with the digger, but I told him I wouldn't. It's not right after what happened as I might disturb evidence, and it will annoy our guests.

Christmas Day is not the day to be driving a noisy machine around."

"I had expected you to clear the site," said Clarence, "but I understand the reason."

"We need to let people leave if they want. Everyone will be scared and might want to go. They're trapped. What if the killer strikes again?" Roy glared at Maddie, but she ignored him.

"Let me ask you both an important question," said Clarence. "You said you had extensive ground works done to sort out drainage, install water lines, and run power to the campsite. You had it landscaped and the trees cut back along with quite a few other jobs. Who did it?"

"Why?" asked Maddie.

"Because I want to know."

"We did most of it ourselves. Bought what we needed and did it. We can't afford to hire anyone. We haven't got that kind of money. What's this about?"

"The man who was killed was from the next village and was a landscape gardener. Did all sorts. He'd do pipes, arrange for other workmen, do gardens, basically anything to do with the land. You didn't employ him?"

"No, we didn't," said Roy. "Look, what are you implying? That we didn't like his work so killed him and made him into a snowman?"

"Just checking facts. No need to get snappy."

"I'll show you snappy." Roy took a step forward.

"Roy!" Maddie grabbed his arm and pulled him back.

"Sorry, but I've had enough of this. I just want a nice Christmas and to be left alone. It's going to be ruined."

"Sorry to bother you." Without another word, Clarence turned and headed back to the campsite. I smiled at the couple, then caught him up.

"Let's have a sit and warm up," I suggested.

"Thanks. I'll take you up on that if you don't mind. First, let's see if Sam's wife has finished in the shower."

We approached the shower block and listened, our exchanged grimace indicating we both felt uncomfortable loitering like this. We couldn't hear any of the three showers running, but there was clattering about and noise inside so Clarence shouted out, "Hello? Can we have a word please? I'm a detective, and I'm with your neighbour. Your husband probably told you about us."

"What do you want?" called out a muffled, nervous voice. "Don't come in! I'm getting dressed."

"We won't enter. Don't worry. I just wanted to ask if you'd seen anything untoward? You were out earlier and we found an important clue. Did you see anyone?"

"Nobody. Please leave me alone. My husband deals with this kind of thing. I have a condition, and I can't talk to strangers. Please, go away."

"I'm sorry, but I do need to ask you a few questions. Are you safe? Not in any trouble?"

"There's no trouble here. We're fine. It's ghastly what happened, but I saw nothing. I keep my head down and don't talk to anyone. Please go."

Clarence and I exchanged a look, but he nodded that he was satisfied, then shouted, "Sorry to disturb you," and we left the poor woman to finish getting dressed.

"She sounded nervous," I noted.

"Sam was right and she's not up to talking to strangers. Some people are like that and get twitchy, even scared. If she has a medical condition, I'm not about to push her too far. We're looking for someone with a lot of bravado and considerable strength anyway."

"The poor woman. It must be terrible for her."

"It must. Now, let's get warm."

Chapter 18

"It's me and Clarence," I called out as we approached the new gazebo. "Nice, isn't it?" I asked the fed-up DI. "My folks chose well. I still can't believe they turned up last night."

"Very kind of them. Max, isn't living like this a nightmare? Look at you all. You're sitting in the cold in a gazebo on Christmas Day when everyone else is lazing on their sofa and enjoying the warmth and maybe a roaring fire. Don't you want a real home?"

"This is a real home. I know what you mean, and of course it would be nice to be sprawled out on a sofa or flicking through the TV channels, but it comes with so many other problems. There will be floors to hoover, kitchens to clean, not that I'd mind that, worries about the cost to heat the house, which would be stressful at Christmas, not to mention the extra food for guests. And don't even get me started on the stuff I used to have. When I packed it up, and sold a lot of it, I couldn't believe the amount of things I'd accumulated. The saddest thing was, I didn't even know I had half of it."

"So, this lifestyle is worth the sacrifice?"

"For me, yes. I'm not saying it's for everyone, and there are certainly things I miss, but the freedom I've gained is worth missing out on a few home comforts. Although, I wish I had a washing machine and a bathroom. Can't have it all." I laughed at the situation, as what else could I do, and realised that even though he was right about the less than ideal situation today, I wouldn't swap it for anything. We were coping, and together, and that was the most important thing. I had all I wanted, and although the circumstances were awful today, there was no way I would have spent so much time outside if I lived in a house. This was perfect, and I loved it!

We entered the new gazebo and I zipped up the door, pleased to find everyone looking comfortable with chairs and blankets and food and drink, just as it should be on Christmas Day.

"You two took your time," grunted Mum like it was an accusation.

"Is everything alright?"

"Of course, love, but you shouldn't wander off without telling us. We were worried."

"And you upset your wife," snapped Dad, shaking his head.

"Min, what's wrong?"

She was sitting cross-legged on the rug with Anxious in her lap, and stroking him repetitively, her eyes unfocused. "You were gone too long. Where were you? I looked but couldn't find you. Max, I was close to freaking out."

"I'm so sorry. We went up to the house and I guess I lost any phone signal there was. Sorry. That was terrible of me. We spoke to everyone again, and this puzzle just keeps getting more difficult."

"I was just being silly, but promise not to go anywhere without us again?"

"I promise. Or at the very least, I'll tell you where I'm going. Now, let's have a drink and I can sort out dinner and explain what we discovered.

Mum sorted drinks—Clarence stuck to orange juice— and we went over what had happened while I readied things in the kitchen.

"I bet it was the owners," said Dad, snaffling a Quality Street in an orange wrapper, much to Mum's disgust as they were her favourites.

"They are definitely acting strange, but now they explained about the snow clearing and why they did it how they did, I'm less inclined to suspect them. It would make no sense." Clarence sipped his juice, frowning as he eyed up the bottles of booze on the table.

"What about this drunk loner?" asked Mum, wrapped up in her red coat, smiling merrily, her cheeks as red as her hair.

"Suspicious, but not unduly so. He's got a history, and is capable of doing terrible things, but I'm afraid to say, and I know this from experience, we all have a monster lurking inside. He was pushed to his limit and responded with violence. That doesn't mean he did this though. My take is that he's trying to get himself together but is struggling."

"Then maybe it was the old couple. Max, you said yourself that when you visited them something was off there." Dad glanced at me and nodded, encouraging me to talk.

"It wasn't much, but yes, like everyone else here, they have secrets. The main issue was David pretending that he forgot he'd been outside in the night. He definitely went out, but now I've had the chance to think about it, I'm sure it was embarrassment as much as anything."

"Why would he be embarrassed about needing a wee?" asked Mum.

"Not that. He was upset because he couldn't remember. My best guess, although I'm not convinced, is that he has a medical condition. Possibly early onset dementia, or Alzheimers, or at least some problem with his short-term memory. Gina was very understanding with him, and didn't push things when he insisted he hadn't been out, which was kind. He was angry because he was convinced he hadn't gone anywhere."

"That's the impression I got too." Clarence had clearly had enough of the juice, so with a raised eyebrow and a nod to the booze, which I nodded back to confirm, he helped himself to a glass of wine and topped everyone up. Seated, and much happier after a sip, he added, "He kept forgetting about the TV and repeatedly turned up the volume crazy high. He's forgetful, and finds it hard to focus for long, so his wife is looking out for him."

"Then who did it?" asked Mum.

"We'll get there. Everything is coming to a head, but there's something we're overlooking. Once we figure out what that is, we'll have our killer."

"It's not that simple, though, is it?" asked Min. "It's not just the killer, it's the fact someone knows who did it. They planted the notebook and the wallet, clearly wanting them to be found and for you to put the pieces together. For whatever reason, they can't come right out and tell you, so are revealing things. Why do that? It means it has to be someone who's staying here, or a local who's hiding around here somewhere. Maybe we should check the outbuildings?"

"I've already done that, but it was tough alone. If we went over things again, and I have permission from Maddie and Roy to look around anywhere I want, maybe we'll discover something. Great idea, Min."

"Thank you." Min beamed, her face flushed, pleased to be more involved after me going off without her.

"But for now let's relax, and unless I'm mistaken, which I'm not, it's about time to eat. Can everyone set things up for dinner? It's a weird time to eat, not quite lunch time, too early for dinner, but I'm starving."

While they sprang into action, and Anxious helpfully carried his empty bowl over to me at the kitchen, causing me to laugh and take pity on him and give him a little taster, I put the finishing touches to things and began plating up.

Once the plates were laden, and with numerous bowls and jars out on the way-too-small coffee table or on the prep table, I served everyone and settled on the blanket next to Min, eyeing my plate greedily.

"Merry Christmas," I said, raising a glass.

"Merry Christmas!"

For a while, nobody spoke, and nobody ate, then Clarence broke the silence by saying, "This looks stunning. Almost too good to eat. Max, I know you said you used to be a top chef, but this is incredible. Did you really do it on the two gas rings?"

"Sure did. It turned out alright, didn't it?"

"Amazing. Thank you so much for the invitation. I feel bad about crashing your party, but, oh boy, am I glad I did."

"You're very welcome. This isn't a day to be alone. It's for friends and family. And you're a friend."

"I really appreciate that. Thank you everyone."

"Can we eat now?" asked Dad, the drool hanging from the corner of his mouth, fork raised, but unsure if he was allowed.

"Of course. Tuck in!"

The beef that'd slow-cooked in my trusty cast-iron pot for hours was succulent, full of flavour, and had provided a beautiful base stock for the soft boiled potatoes. Having thought I'd need multiple pots despite my vow to do one-pot cooking, I discovered that the single large, some would say oversized, pot worked perfectly to do the potatoes and the veg, and I even managed to do the stuffing in a special way that cooked it through.

As the beef rested and the potatoes and veg steamed in a bowl, I reduced the stock to a thick, unctuous gravy, then for the last ten minutes I had the heat up high after decanting the dark nectar and browned off the potatoes and the stuffing. The result? Christmas Dinner with a twist, and a flavour-packed punch everyone enjoyed and happily had a second helping of.

By the time we'd finished, even Anxious had given up and had resorted to lying on his side, his belly extended and worryingly close to popping like an over-inflated balloon, and the rest of us weren't in much better condition.

Dad basically force-fed Mum cheese and crackers while we drank coffee and tried not to move, and it was perfect. We chatted, laughed, complained in a good-natured way about our stomachs and issues with belts, and savoured the atmosphere, the outside world forgotten for a while.

Once I felt able, I insisted on clearing up the kitchen, everyone but Clarence letting me get on with it. The merry detective didn't understand that I enjoyed this part of cooking, so repeatedly offered to help until Dad explained to him that as bizarre as it might seem, I loved tidying up and putting my kitchen back into the shape I preferred, teasing me about tea towels and crockery placement good-naturedly, until Clarence ceded and left me to it.

As I wiped, organised, and generally pottered about, happy to be standing and at least burning off a few calories, I let the events of the day play out. There was a lot to think about and plenty of concerns, but I felt that familiar tingle at the base of my neck and the just-out-of-reach sensation of the answer being there but not quite able to surface yet. I'd get there, I knew I would, and soon the detective and I would have to brave the elements and check a few things out, but also ensure the others were involved. Searching the outbuildings was a good idea, and might lead to more clues, but I was now convinced the answer lay elsewhere and only by being outside would the truth reveal itself.

What was I missing here? Why would a landscape gardener who lived not too far away be up here and killed in such a horrific way? What point was there to such a display? Did someone hate Christmas that much? Hate him? Why allow him to be discovered at all? Why risk capture by planting him in the middle of a campsite?

It was perplexing, and annoying, as the logic of it eluded me, but I'd learned that often there was no logic to what people did and they simply acted out of a madness that consumed them and left little room for common sense.

As I pegged out the tea towel and the dishcloth, I had an epiphany of sorts and at least part of the puzzle clicked into place. Could that be right? Surely not? It was far-fetched even for me, so was this a mere fancy brought on by too much food, way more alcohol throughout the day than I was used to, although I felt like my head was clear, or was this the answer we'd been searching for?

There was only one way to find out, but I knew that merely confronting the possible killer wasn't enough. I had to find out more about the why, and even the how, before I took things further.

Mulling it over, I realised the room was silent, and as I turned to the others, it was with confusion that I studied their faces.

"Why are you all standing up? Has something happened?"

"Max, we're standing because we were worried. Nobody said anything as we didn't want to break your concentration, but you've been stock still for at least five minutes. And why are you holding a Jaffa Cake?" Min stepped closer, then put a hand to my arm, and asked with a concerned smile, "Are you going to eat that or is it for display purposes only?"

I studied the sweet treat that'd caused so much controversy over the years regards if it was a biscuit or a cake—it's a cake, it even says so in the name—then wolfed it with a sheepish grin. "Wow, they're good. Sorry to worry you. I was thinking about the case. I think we should go now and check out the buildings. It'll be dark soon, and we don't want to be out then. We need to do this right away and catch the killer."

"You know, don't you?" asked Min, shaking her head. "I can't believe it! Again?" Exasperated, she wrung her hands as she chewed on her lip.

"What's wrong?"

"I wanted to help solve it. You always beat me to it."

"Not always, and look, I have a hunch, nothing more, but I could be wrong. Let's talk later, and please don't ask any more questions. I don't want to put ideas in your head."

"Don't you owe it to us to explain what you think you know?" asked Clarence. "Max, you're a great guy, and I can't thank you and your family enough for everything you've done today, but please don't forget that I'm a police officer, a DI, and I am running this investigation. Surely you should tell me what you think?"

"That's not how our Max does his investigating. He always waits, or ropes us in once he's closing in on the killer," crowed Dad, looking proud as punch.

"That's as maybe, but—"

"No buts," insisted Dad.

"You leave Max to do his thing," ordered Mum.

"Guys, it's fine. Clarence, it's just an idea, nothing certain. I'm not saying I know with a hundred percent certainty, but it's a strong hunch. A few things have led me to this, and of course I'll tell you if you want."

"Fine, have it your way." He smiled at me, dropped his shoulders, and asked, "Any chance of a Jaffa Cake?"

Everyone laughed, and even cheered, so after one each, we prepared to brave the cold and see if we could finally figure out this perplexing mystery once and for all.

As usual it took a while, in no small part because of my wacky mother. Actually, it was entirely down to her. Not only did she have to re-do her make-up just in case she had to talk to anyone, but her hair needed spraying, so it involved a trip back to their motorhome, then she had to get a different pair of socks for her red wellies, then she spent an age faffing with her bandanna, and after we thought we were finally good to go, she insisted on packing a light picnic in case anyone got peckish.

"Love, we're literally going to the top of the campsite," explained Dad with the patience of a saint. "We don't need a picnic or nibbles or drinks or any of that."

"We might get stranded," growled Mum, daring him to defy her with one of her steely looks.

"If we do, which we won't, we can always make it back here."

"What if there's another snowstorm and we get trapped in a barn? We'll need our supplies then."

"Fine, but you're carrying it," sighed Dad.

"I can't carry it. It'll mess with the lines of my coat, and it's really heavy."

"Then don't pack so much!" Mum smiled sweetly and batted her eyes, and Dad caved like he always did, so with a sigh, and yet smiling at Mum, he said, "Then I guess I'll be carrying it, won't I?" and took the pack from her.

Winking at me, Mum ordered, "Lead the way," and knowing better than to argue, I whistled for Anxious who groaned but was up like a shot and waiting at the door, so I unzipped the sturdy fabric and shivered as a blast of icy air tore through me.

"Here we go," I sighed, then stepped out into yet another blizzard.

Chapter 19

Night would soon be here, crashing down in an instant like it always did at this time of the year. How I longed for the summer months when I could sit out in shorts, feeling smug and warm, until ten at night and get myself off to bed with birds still singing, rather than in the middle of the afternoon.

But it was Christmas, I had my family with me, and despite our rather gruesome task I felt good about life and optimistic regards the future. Min and I had snuggled up all night, rather than me trying to fit into the claustrophobic pop-top roof bed that I couldn't imagine was designed for anyone over twelve. We might not be back where we should be, but we were getting there, and the advent of a new year brought with it all kinds of hope. Spring would be here in a few months, and by March we usually had warm days. I couldn't wait.

Right now, I still had to contend with an atrocious blizzard, my parents, and a murderer on the loose. As my folks bickered and Mum kept badgering Clarence about police business, I wasn't sure which was the most testing, but knew I had to stop getting distracted or we'd have to wait until tomorrow to try to resolve this terrible situation.

A door slammed and I turned to catch a brief glimpse of long blond hair as a shadowy figure ducked back into Sam's motorhome. Raised voices from inside, then Christmas jingles played and laughter broke out. Whatever the argument had been was clearly over and the children squealed and the baby cried. Cramped conditions must be hard on families, especially at this time of year.

Dad struggled under the weight of the backpack Mum had rammed with food along with whatever else she deemed necessary, mostly her make-up and shoes and a few spare bandannas, but he still managed to help her through the deepening snow. Clarence led the way, everyone else following in single file behind, the going easier for Anxious who brought up the rear, refusing to be carried now we were on an important mission.

Maddie had clearly heeded our concerns and had cleared a large section around the entrance, meaning once roads in town were passable the police could make it up here. Still far from ideal, it was a start, and I wondered how long it would be before teams arrived to give Clarence some much-needed support. The poor guy had a lot to handle up here alone, but he seemed capable and I liked him, although I had to remind myself that he had issues and I was certain that when alone he'd be hitting the booze hard.

Kicking through the slush was a delight after the snow, and we spread out, our spirits lifting, as we approached the first outbuilding. Along with several ancient stone barns in the same style as the house, there was a more modern agricultural building of steel and wood once used to house cattle, now long defunct. Although large, it only took a few minutes to search as there was nothing but machinery and a few stacks of straw bales home to mice, the rest of the space empty.

Rather than try to cram into the barns together, we split up, with Clarence taking my folks—praise be!—and Min and I teaming up with Anxious who led the way, nose to the ground, tail spinning fast as he finally had the chance to follow the trails.

He seemed to hit on something almost immediately, and was snorting like a pig under an oak tree as he zigzagged back and forth then suddenly barked and ran inside without glancing up and careened into a snowdrift then vanished.

"Anxious!" Min darted forward and I was hot on her heels. The snow was four feet high and he could be killed in there, so I frantically scrabbled in the snow like Min before she found him and hauled him out. "You silly boy!"

Anxious grinned, then licked her face manically before shaking in her arms, flinging snow everywhere.

"That was a close one. Be careful in here. The door's so rotten it's almost off the hinges and there's a lot of junk around, so watch for sharp metal. Anxious, no running off."

He looked sad for a millisecond, then barked again, so Min released him once we'd got past the drift and we each took a moment to survey the room once I'd flicked on the lights. Piles of timber, random gates in all sizes, furniture half-covered with dusty blue tarps, and endless pieces of rusting machinery meant it was a real chore to search the room, but eventually we gave it up as a lost cause, and had found nothing. Yet Anxious continued to bark randomly, without actually homing in on anything, and was left as confused as us.

"What is it, boy? What's in here?" I asked, exchanging a look with Min.

"He definitely thinks there's something here we should know about." Min led him around the cluttered space, and every so often he'd bark and stop to sniff something, but then he'd shake his head and move on, unable to find what he was looking for.

Suddenly I understood, and tapped Min's arm then pointed up. Slowly, our eyes drifted towards the oak roof truss covered in woodworm but so thick and solid that it would be only cosmetic. Beams like that would outlast the building itself.

Anxious sat underneath the truss and wagged merrily, dust billowing as his excitement grew and he yipped that we'd finally understood.

Min gasped. I removed my hat and scratched at my head, surprised to feel my hair after what felt like a lifetime of scratchy wool.

"Is that what I think it is?" she asked.

"If you think it's a bloody chain, then yes, it is."

"No need for foul language. Sorry, that was in bad taste. Max, why is that chain wrapped around the beam?"

"I guess it was used to haul up engines or some such. It's fixed to the thingamajig. The pulley thing. I don't know the name for it. A hoist, I guess. Look, there are all manner of old parts, so maybe this used to be a workshop for fixing vehicles and farm machinery." With the cold getting into my bones, I stomped my feet to warm up, surprised to hear a hollow sound beneath us.

"A secret bunker?" Min's eyes were wide and her cheeks were flushed even in the low light, her excitement growing.

"Let's take a look. I bet I know what it is. An inspection pit to work on vehicles. It would explain the hoist. Anxious, mind out of the way, please. Min, can you give me a hand?"

"You bet!" With Anxious growing bored now the dumb humans had finally figured out what he'd been telling us all along, he wandered off for a nose around while we inspected the floor.

Although we'd made quite a mess of things traipsing around, there were clear signs of a disturbance as the oil and grime had been scraped by heavy boots, and as we explored the edges I noted a clean patch so we bent to study the floor.

"It's just thick boards covering it over. Want to move it?" asked Min.

"Maybe we should call for Clarence. He'll want to see this, and we don't want to destroy any evidence."

"We've done a good job of that already. Max, why is there a massive chain with blood on it? Assuming it is blood. It's hanging there like it was used to haul someone up. Could that be right?"

"It might explain some of the rips on Mitchell's Santa suit, and maybe the reason he was so torn up on his back lies beneath the floor. I'll get Clarence."

"Hurry. I don't like it in here. It's like a torture chamber."

"Hang tight, or come with me. Anxious will protect you, but maybe we shouldn't split up."

Neither took much convincing, so we rushed outside only to find Clarence looking despondent with Mum and Dad either side regaling him with a tale I'd heard many times before about how they won a dance marathon and got free admission for life to their favourite weekly jive session. Poor guy looked ready to bolt, but brightened when he saw us and hurried forward, leaving my folks oblivious and still talking.

"Having fun?" I chuckled.

"They like to talk. A lot." Clarence took me by the arm and led me away before asking, "Please tell me you found something. There's nothing in the other buildings, and I'm beginning to think this is a wild goose chase. We need something to push this thing forward and catch this maniac. Max, the longer this goes on, the less chance there is of solving it. Give me some good news."

"I'm not sure it's good news as such, but there is something in the barn. We were coming to get you, as we didn't want to disturb anything."

"Great! That's great." Smiling, Clarence turned to my folks and asked them to wait outside while he looked at something with us. Of course, they would hear none of it and before he'd even finished talking they'd both barged past him and walked straight into the snowdrift, ending up in a tangled heap with Anxious jumping about on them as what an awesome game this had become.

"Are they always so chatty?" asked Clarence as he studied the wriggling pair, eyes appealing for me to do something.

"Pretty much, yeah. They like to be involved. To help, as they would put it."

"Interfere, is how I'd put it. Okay, how about you show us what you found? Min, is everything okay?"

"Yes. I'm concerned about what's in here, but I'm fine. Let us show you the chain, and we think there's an inspection pit."

"Intriguing." Wasting no time, he followed Min over to the thick chain then took his time inspecting the winch system and the various vehicle parts, trying his best to preserve what was likely a crime scene. I had a quick word with Mum and Dad and they actually stayed back, finally understanding the importance of what was happening.

After plenty of photos and another wander around the building, we gathered at the edge of the fake floor and I helped Clarence to lift up the boards. They were heavy, and had been fixed together, so it was awkward with everyone milling about, but we eventually managed to slide the boards free.

"It's empty." Clarence's disappointment was obvious, and I felt the same way, and Min stepped to the edge and peered inside.

"I was sure there would be something inside."

"Me too," I admitted. "But we still have the chain and pulley and it does look like blood on the chain. What do we think happened here?"

"Are you all serious?" asked Dad, barging past Clarence and taking centre stage right beside the chain. He reached up and tugged at it with his gloved hand, the mechanism moving freely, the winch clearly capable of hoisting a man up.

"I'm not following." Clarence's frustration with my folks was clearly building, but he didn't ask Dad to let go or to move, as Dad seemed very confident about something, and was grinning.

"Me either."

"Jack, will you tell us?" asked Min sweetly, rolling her eyes at me and smiling. She knew what he was like, and now he had everyone's attention he'd milk this for all it was worth.

"Aw, sweetie, of course I will." Dad tugged on the chain again, letting it feed through his hands, causing Clarence to cough to hide his frustration.

We waited, but Dad just grinned until Anxious barked for him to get on with it.

"Tell us then," I encouraged.

"These winches are really strong. They're for engines. But I bet it hasn't been used for anything like that in years. It's not greased properly, and it's filthy apart from where someone has used it recently. They'll most likely be covered in oil from it. There was oil and terrible wounds on the dead bloke, right?"

"Yes, but it could have been from any number of things," said Clarence.

"Or, it was from being wrapped up in chain and strung up like a set of Christmas lights. Why do they never come back out of the box easily? They're always tangled and it's so frustrating."

"You're getting sidetracked, love," said Mum.

"Um, yes, sorry. Where was I? Ah, yes. The dead guy was strung up and I bet he got a beating. Maybe you should check his body for such things. But see, the problem with these winches, especially the old ones, is you have to know what you're doing or things can get pretty hairy very quickly. You can get tangled, or they drop, especially if it's faulty. Our guy was winched up, something went wrong with the system, and he got mangled and I bet the killer just lost the plot and did the deed. He could have used anything in here to kill him, or maybe he died from the wound to his back."

"The winch seems solid to me," I said.

"Oh yeah? Watch this." Dad grabbed the chain and pulled, causing it to raise the other section, but then something cracked and the whole thing spun wildly, the chain tangled, and he had to jump aside before he got garrotted. "See?" he said smugly, wiping a bead of sweat from his forehead. "Blimey, that was close," he giggled.

"I think we've seen enough. Maybe this was where Mitchell was killed, but it doesn't help us with our investigation. Not unless there's something else, Jack?"

"The rest is up to you." Dad spread his hands, beaming at us like he'd solved the case, but all this had done was lead to more confusion.

"How did the killer get the body out into the field?" I wondered, more to myself than the others.

"He dragged him or used something as a makeshift sledge. Maybe he even had a proper sledge." Again, Dad grinned, enjoying himself immensely. "But what I'm thinking is this wasn't meant to happen. I think it's more a case of a beating going too far and things getting way out of hand. That's what I think, anyway."

Mum clapped, then kissed Dad, who beamed with pride.

"You might be right, but we still need to know who did it, and why? Max, I think it's time we heard from you." Clarence nodded for me to speak up, and although reticent, I knew there was little point in delaying things any longer. It was a hunch, nothing more, but after finding this winch I was more certain than ever that I knew at least some of what was going on, but plenty still eluded me.

"You have to understand that this is conjecture, nothing more. Let me give you my reasons, and see what you think. We need a plan to get this to play out, and for that to happen we'll have to work as a team and possibly get the others involved too. Will that be okay, Clarence?"

"If it gets us our killer without risking anyone getting hurt, then of course we can do it. But if it gets dangerous, I'm calling it off. Nothing is worth losing a life over."

"Then I better tell you who I think did it." Reluctantly, I took to the floor as Dad moved to the side, coughed to clear my throat, then paused for a moment as I tried to figure out how to best express what I believed was going on, and how this explained so much of the strange behaviour we'd witnessed on this most festive of days.

Chapter 20

"Unless I'm very wrong about this, I think the killer is..." I paused at the sound of a commotion from outside, much to everyone's dismay, but they heard it too and we hurried to the door as the last of the day slipped away. It didn't matter, as the whole area was lit up like a Christmas tree.

Scores of lanterns, torches, phones, and yes, even Christmas tree lights shone brightly, held by a horde of Santas. It was the most surreal sight I'd ever witnessed, and for a moment I thought I was seeing things.

"It's not just me, is it? They are really there, aren't they?" I asked Min, taking her hand as she gnawed at her lip.

"It's real. What are they doing?"

"You better leave this to me," said Clarence, stepping forward as the crowd spotted us.

"Don't they look lovely?" cooed Mum, smiling at us.

"Mum, can't you hear them? They're baying for blood."

"What are they chanting, dearie? Is it a Christmas carol? I do love a carol."

"You daft pilchard," said Dad, tutting. "They're saying they want to know who the killer is. They're out for revenge."

"Why would they want revenge? The poor dead man isn't even from the village, is he?"

"No, but some people probably knew him and he only lived a few miles away. Assuming they even know who was killed. But I think the alcohol and everyone getting worked up in the pub is more to blame for this reaction." I hurried to join Clarence who was now surrounded by angry Santas shouting at him or the world in general.

"I told you I don't know. Everyone needs to go home."

"You do know," shouted one of the men I'd seen earlier. "You know who the killer is and you aren't telling us. Where is he? Have you locked him up yet? We can't have a killer on the loose around here. People have kids. It's Christmas. You need to do something. If you don't know, then we're going to find out. It has to be one of the people staying here."

The crowd cheered that he was right, and that they were going to solve this case before anyone else died, their ire rising to dangerous levels thanks to booze and mob mentality.

Clarence raised his arms and waved as he shouted, "Everyone, calm down. Please go back to your homes. This is not helping. Do you think this is how I want to spend my day? I had a microwave lasagne ready and waiting and a bottle of Jack, but instead I've been traipsing up and down that hill in the snow, wandering around a frozen wasteland, and the only thing that's kept me sane are these lovely people." He waved at us and nodded to me, but his words weren't having the desired effect and if anything the Santas were getting angrier.

"You should do your job," shouted an old man in a suit that had seen better days.

"Yeah, what are we paying you for?" demanded a nice-looking lady in an immaculate costume complete with beard.

"In case nobody has noticed, it's been snowing all day and no other officers have made it. I'm getting close to solving this, but you being here is not helping. Go home," bellowed Clarence, losing his temper.

"We will not. We deserve to know what's been going on. How close are you to finding the killer?" shouted the man who seemed to be the unofficial leader of this group.

"That's police business. Leave now."

"We want justice," they chanted, pumping their arms and stomping their feet as the cold settled into them now they weren't marching up the hill and were sobering up.

"Anxious, care to do the honours?" I asked the little guy as I squatted beside him.

He'd always despised arguments or raised voices of any kind, and would go off and hide if possible, but this was clearly too intriguing for him and he was handling it well, although he was shaking and his ears were down, clearly close to making a break for it.

With a nod to him that it was okay, I readied for what was coming, then stepped away as an ear-splitting howl filled the night, vibrating on a level that caused everyone to shriek and slap their hands over their ears. Thankfully, I'd already covered mine after pulling my hat down, but it still sent a shiver down my spine.

The moment Anxious stopped, mostly because I gave him a biscuit, I stepped forward beside Clarence and addressed the crowd. "You're scaring everyone. What were you thinking coming here like this? It's Christmas, and we've been outside all day trying to help Clarence solve this terrible crime. You've been in the pub, at your homes having dinner, and playing with children and enjoying yourselves. Now you come here after a lovely day and start demanding answers like you deserve them when you didn't lift a finger to help. Did any of you even think to bring food or drink for us? No, of course you didn't. You got drunk after dinner and worked yourselves into a frenzy but now you're freezing, like we've been for hours, and you should leave."

"Now!" bellowed Min, nodding to me that she had my back.

Stifling a smirk, I smiled at the love of my life as the others joined us and we stood in a defensive line, barricading the Santas from moving into the campsite, leaving them shuffling their feet, blowing on their hands, and shivering as none of them were prepared for the weather. Santa might wear thermal clothes, but their cheap polyester knock-offs were not genuine winter attire and they were just now realising this.

As an embarrassed silence fell over them, the young barmaid stepped forward and tentatively asked Clarence, "How's your head?"

"Much better, thank you."

"Great. And can you please tell us if you're any closer to figuring this out? I know we've behaved badly, but we do want to help, and we'd love to know what's happening. Sorry for not coming earlier, and we should have brought supplies. At least some hot toddies and maybe some cold cuts. Although, it's cold enough already," she laughed, smiling at Clarence. "You're so brave. All of you are."

There were murmurs of agreement, and then things got truly weird as the crowd that moments ago seemed ready to lynch us now started clapping, their mood switching. We were rather taken aback and unsure what to do, so stood there like actors at the final curtain call. My folks actually bowed like they'd solved the crime of the century, rather than being utterly in the dark about what had happened.

Clarence left us for a few minutes while he spoke quietly with the shivering Santas, then returned as they left, much to everyone's relief.

"Shouldn't the owners have come out to see what was happening?" asked Min. "And where are the other guests? Surely everyone would have heard that?"

As if on cue, Maddie and Roy exited the cabin, wrapped up and shining torches at the retreating figures. "What happened?" asked Roy. "We had the TV up loud, then the adverts came on and I got up for a cuppa and heard shouting."

"Just some disgruntled Santas come to disturb the peace," said Clarence.

"The ones from the pub?" asked Maddie. "Sorry, yes, obviously from the pub. Are you all okay?"

We told her we were, and that it was over now, but as they turned to leave, I asked, "Do you mind staying? I was about to tell the others what I think happened, and it might be a good idea if you stay too. Maybe you can go and check on your guests, tell them there's something they all need to hear. Do you mind?"

"Of course not. We feel terrible that you've been out in the weather trying to figure this out, and we're sorry we've been rather off. The truth is we're exhausted, overwhelmed, and really wanted to try to enjoy today. We should have helped more. We wish we had. We're so sorry."

Clarence put their minds at ease by telling them it was fine, and that this was finally coming to a head. I caught the look in his eyes and knew he'd worked out at least part of this conundrum just like me, but was playing his cards close to his chest.

Maddie and Roy went ahead into the campsite to round up anyone who was willing to come outside, while the rest of us grouped close together, all eyes on me and Clarence.

"Come on, spill it!" insisted Min, tugging at my arm.

"Let's hear it, Son," said Dad. "You left us hanging there and that's not nice."

"There's no time now. We need to hurry and ensure nobody leaves. I can hear a vehicle. Quick."

As an engine disturbed the silence of the night, we hastily made our way back into the snow-covered field, the going easier but the ground becoming treacherous as it iced over.

As we turned into the hidden field, the old motorhome owned by Gina and David came spluttering towards us belching smoke, the tires skidding on the snow, but making slow progress.

"I'll stop them!" said Dad, dashing ahead and waving his arms to halt the vehicle.

Before they could run him over, the vehicle skidded to a stop and David jumped out. "What are you doing, you mad fool?" he snapped, glancing at Dad then the rest of us.

"You can't leave. You're both suspects in a murder." Dad put his hands on his hips, lit up by the headlights like a Christmas decoration, daring David to defy him.

"Leave this to me, please." Clarence took David to one side and had a quiet word. David got back into the cab, discussed things with his wife, then they trudged over to us.

"This better be good," grumbled Gina. "We want to go home now the roads should be clear. This has been a very stressful day."

"Or you want to escape your crime," bellowed Mum, shoving past Dad to wag a finger at the startled couple.

"How dare you!? We aren't killers."

"No? Then why is David sneaking around in the night then pretending he couldn't remember?"

"Mum, calm down. Remember what I told you? David might just be rather forgetful and didn't want to discuss it. You shouldn't be so confrontational."

"Max is right," admitted David. "I should have said. Gina thought it would be nice for us to come away and escape the questions and sympathy from the family, but the truth is I'm becoming forgetful. It's a real concern, and I'm sorry if I caused any problems."

"You don't need to explain yourself to these strangers," said Gina as she put her arm around David then whispered in his ear. He nodded, then she told us, "He's not been well. The break has done him good. He's no killer."

"What about you?" accused Dad. "Maybe you snuck out and did the deed?"

"Dad, remember you said Mitchell was strung up with the hoist? I doubt Gina is up to that. And he had to be moved to the field too."

"Oh yes, right."

"Can we please get on?" asked Clarence. "I believe I have an idea about who did this, but I'm not sure I even believe my own mind at this point. This day has been way too long, and it's too surreal. Max, are you with me?"

"I am. Let's go."

Without waiting, Clarence headed into the field with everyone following, and once there we found Maddie and Roy with Kev, the loner, and Sam, the family man, waiting right where the snowman had been.

They watched us approach silently; everyone looked nervous, cold, and scared. Nothing was said until we were grouped in a loose circle, all the players present bar a few, and those who were missing were the most important ones of all.

"They aren't coming, are they?" whispered Clarence.

"I doubt it. You figured it out too?"

"Some of it. I'm not sure it makes sense, but it's the only explanation that I can think of."

"It's rude to whisper," lectured Mum, wagging a finger.

"Sorry," we both said, then turned to Sam.

"Why are you both looking at me like that? What's going on?"

"What's your job, Sam?" I asked.

"Job? I'm between work at the moment. Had a hard year and decided to take some time off. I always liked it around here, so figured a break would be good for us."

"And by us, you mean?"

Sam frowned. "The family, obviously."

"What were the issues you had, Sam?" asked Clarence, barely a whisper.

"Private. None of you business."

"Issues at home, maybe?" I suggested. "But let me guess, your previous work involved vehicle repairs, didn't it? A mechanic maybe?"

"How did you know?"

"Call it a hunch, or call it the fact you have oil under your nails and knew how to work an old engine hoist."

Mum and Dad gasped, Min gripped my arm tight, but the others just listened, not understanding where this was going.

"If you must know, I had my own business repairing classic cars. So, yes, always rather oily."

"But that's not why you wanted a break, is it? You may as well tell us. We know what you did."

"Look, what's the meaning of this? I want to get back to my family. It's cold, dark, and I don't like where this is headed."

"You can't get back to your family, can you?" I asked, feeling bad for doing this but not knowing how else to get the answers we needed.

"Course I can. They're inside."

"Then please go and get them," said Clarence, his voice wavering as if uncertain about what he now believed.

"Fine, I'll get Jo, but I'm not dragging the kids out to face this. You've got no right to do this, you know," he told Clarence.

"Please get your wife, then this will all be over."

"I will!" In a huff, Sam marched back towards his van.

"Blimey, for a minute there I thought you guys were saying it was that dude who killed the snowman," laughed Kev, wobbling a little, and clearly having been drinking substantially.

"Just wait," I told him.

"Max, you don't think it was his wife, do you?" asked Min. Then something clicked and she moved very close and asked, "Ah, I get it now. Wow, could he really have done that?"

"I think so."

"Hey, what are you talking about?" asked Mum as she and Dad got close, hating to miss out.

"Hello?" came the high-pitched voice of Jo, Sam's elusive wife.

"Can we have a word, please?" called Clarence.

Jo, wrapped up in a thick coat, hat, gloves, scarf, and loose trousers, stood on the steps just outside the door, her long blond hair covering her face. "I'm not good with strangers. I want to go back inside. Sam said you wanted to see me, and now you have."

"Closer, please," said Clarence.

"No, and you can't make me. Why won't you leave us alone?"

"Is everything alright, ma'am?" he asked. "Are you in danger?"

"No, I'm fine. Leave us alone!" With that, she turned, entered the van, then slammed the door shut.

"I have absolutely no idea what is going on here, but I like it," laughed Kev.

"Do we know who did it yet?" Mum asked Dad, who shrugged.

"Don't think so, love. At least, we don't. Max and Clarence seem to believe it was Sam though. Is that right, Max?"

"Get ready to storm the van on my command," said Clarence, and then the door banged open and Sam marched over, looking furious.

"You made my wife cry, you terrified my children, and the young one will never settle now. Look what you did."

"No, Sam, look what you did. Why? What possessed you? And why lie about your family?" Then I understood, and my tone softened as I saw the telltale signs in his eyes. The signs of a madman. He wasn't just a little unwell, he was clearly very ill indeed.

"I… You don't understand. None of you do. Leave us be. I want to go home. I want to be with my family."

"But they aren't here, are they?" I asked.

"Max, you're making no sense," said Dad. "We just saw his wife, and we've heard the family on and off all day."

"Have we, or have we heard the same music, the same singing, and the same laughter repeatedly? Think about it. I mean, really think about it. They aren't here."

"But his wife was just outside," insisted Mum.

"Anxious, fetch the lady," I told him, waving a biscuit in front of his nose.

He tore off and darted between Sam's legs, his pom-pom bouncing, the little bell tinkling, then raced up the steps and launched at the handle, pulling it open before dropping down and dashing inside. Sam turned to give chase, but I grabbed his arm.

"Let me go!"

"It's over," I told him.

"I've done nothing wrong."

With a yip, Anxious raced back from the van and over to us where he dropped a long blond wig at my feet then fixed his eyes on the real prize.

I patted his head, handed over the biscuit, then stood with the wig in my hand.

"Sam's alone here, and always has been. Sam, I assume you separated from your family and it was too much for you? How long has this been going on? I'm guessing your wife had an affair with Mitchell, and that's why you killed him?"

Sam sank to his knees and sobbed.

For him at least, the worst was finally over.

A mighty gasp came from behind us and everyone turned to find an astonished gaggle of Santas wide-eyed and dumbstruck.

I caught the attention of the de facto leader; he shrugged and admitted, "We didn't want to miss anything."

Chapter 21

Clarence ushered the nosy Santas away, promising he'd explain later this evening in the pub, as he certainly deserved a drink. Once they'd departed, the rest of us gathered around a despondent Sam as Clarence read him his rights. Min took pity on the poor man and put an arm around him, so Mum joined her as no way was she missing out on cuddle time even if it was with an unhinged killer.

"Why don't you tell us everything?" encouraged Min with a warm smile.

"It'll make you feel better," beamed Mum. "Unburden yourself. After all, you're going to prison anyway, so you may as well explain. Lighten the load. Ask for forgiveness."

"I'll never ask for forgiveness, but you're right, I might as well tell you. I'm so sorry, everyone. I ruined Christmas, when you just wanted a nice time. I couldn't help it though. I had to come, and everything fell apart. I don't think I'm very well."

"You knew this campsite already, didn't you?" asked Clarence.

"I did. We used to come every year for Christmas with the children. They're teenagers now, plus the youngster, and we've been coming for at least a decade. Things hadn't been right with me and Jo for a long time, but we stuck together for the sake of the family, but after the baby it all turned sour. I lost my business, she was always busy with the children, and we grew apart."

"That's sad, but it happens," said Clarence. "I'm assuming she had an affair, or at least a fling, with Mitchell. Is that right?"

"She did. It was the worst day of my life. Last year while we were here, and on Christmas Day if you can believe it, she finally admitted that she'd been carrying on with him for a year. They'd met in town, got on, and ever since then they'd been meeting up and laughing at me."

"Son, they wouldn't do that," soothed Dad with a sympathetic pat of Sam's head which made him frown in confusion.

"They would and they did! They had an affair. She admitted it. I got the truth out of her and once we got home we separated. He broke it off with her a few months later, said it was too intense, and he couldn't handle it. I heard it all through her friends. I hardly get to see my kids, the baby doesn't even know me, and everything is ruined."

"So you decided to get revenge?" I asked.

"Every year I'd dress as Santa for the kids and we had a great time here. I even had the recording of the last year here when we were a happy family. That's what you heard playing. I had it on repeat." Sam's eyes lost focus and his attention drifted, then he hung his head.

"Tell us. It's for the best, Sam."

He shuddered, looked me in the eye, and whispered, "I think I lost my mind somewhere along the way. I don't even know where the wig came from or the idea of pretending Jo was still with me. I'm not well, I know that now. I need help. I think I wanted to get caught anyway. I found myself with Mitchell's stuff in my hands right where I left him, and just dropped things. Like I was Jo trying to get me caught. It's like I'm two people. Clarence, I'm sorry I attacked you. I panicked. But then my head cleared and I covered you with the blanket. I'm an utter mess!" Sam sobbed into Mum's shoulder, and she stroked his head, but even she knew it would take more than that to fix this man broken by life turning out so differently to how he'd expected.

"Sam, that's your name, right?" asked Kev, clearly confused by the turn of events but tipsy enough to be blunt.

"Yes, and you are?"

"I'm Kev, your neighbour. Let me get this straight. You dressed up as your wife and pranced about the campsite, and even fooled the DI and everyone else?"

"I guess. I wanted people to think we were still a family."

I studied Sam, wondering how much of his grief was real, and if he really was insane, or pretending now he'd been caught. I had to ask a few questions, though, my inquisitive nature meant I had no choice, so after a deep breath asked, "Why the snowman, Sam? Why not leave after you'd killed him?"

"I couldn't get away, could I? I didn't know where to put the body or what to do, so figured if I buried him in a snowman he'd be hidden for a few days until the snow cleared enough to leave."

"He really is nuts," said Dad.

"Jack, that's not nice," warned Min.

"I'm just telling it like it is. Fella's got a few screws loose. Snowmen to hide corpses? That's bonkers. Dressing up as Santa for his missing family. And why'd you put the dead bloke in the Santa outfit anyway?"

"I, er, went to his house and clobbered him. He was out cold and I dressed him up and was going to make him suffer for what he did. I loaded him into the van, but I guess I must have panicked and I drove off with the back doors open and he got tangled with the rope and was dragged along for a while. I put him back in after a few seconds, but he was already quite injured. When I was here, I was surprised to find he wasn't as bad as I'd thought, so got him into the barn and strung him up on the engine winch and had a word."

"You mean you beat him, don't you?" I asked.

"Might have given him a few slaps," mumbled Sam, wiping his eyes. "I got carried away and he ended up dead. I hid him in the barn but began to worry he'd be found as Maddie and Roy, and you seem lovely by the way, were so busy with their renovations. When it began to snow in the night, I snuck out and dragged him back here then you know the rest."

"I think it's time to go," said Clarence kindly, nodding to me to help.

Sam was a broken man. Unstable, and in desperate need of care. We guided him back to his van and gathered a few things, then I helped Clarence get him up to the farmhouse where Roy was waiting after offering to drive down into the village. Clarence said he'd wait there for help to arrive and inform everyone in the pub what had happened.

Watching them drive away, I had the strangest feeling that something still wasn't right, but couldn't figure out what that might have been. Then it clicked into place, and with my head torch to guide the way, I returned to the others now nervously drinking wine outside Vee. Anxious looked up from his spot in Min's lap, but snuggled down and closed his eyes again. Mum and Dad were full of sympathy for Sam, but stoked I'd helped solve the crime yet again.

"What's up, Son?" asked Dad.

"I need to check Vee. I haven't done it since yesterday and I have the weirdest feeling."

"About what?" asked Min, chewing her lip.

"Remember in Cornwall and the graffiti on the van?"

"Course I do."

"We haven't looked recently."

With a nod, Min lowered Anxious to the rug and then the four of us used our torches to inspect Vee. There was no extra artwork on the driver's side, but on the passenger side, right at the back of the van, was more graffiti in the same style as before. Swirling lines in black, white, and orange to match the two-tone colour scheme of Vee were beautiful, but as on the other side, incomplete.

"What's that all about then?" asked Dad with a frown.

"They shouldn't be defacing your lovely van like that," growled Mum, glancing around like we'd catch the vandal in the act.

"Actually, I like it," I beamed.

"Me too," agreed Min. "It's bright and cheery, and I think it's trying to tell us something."

"Like what?" I wondered, and not for the first time.

"Who knows? But I don't think it's malicious. Maybe one day it will be a completed piece of art and we'll understand, but for now can we just drink our wine while you explain just how you figured out it was Sam that did this?"

"Now that's a great idea," I laughed, squeezing her hand which I hadn't even realised I was holding.

"Once settled, and with Anxious now in my lap, I explained how I'd begun to get suspicious of Sam after we spoke to his "wife" at the showers. Something seemed off, even though both I and Clarence were convinced it really was her. If nothing else, Sam was an expert at impersonating a woman because of his slender frame and high-pitched voice. Plus, we had never actually seen her face.

"Yes, but why were you suspicious?" asked Dad.

"Because when we were going back I thought I heard her voice from inside the van, but she wasn't in there yet. That led me to thinking maybe it was a recording, and the next few times we passed I paid attention and it was the same. At least, I was mostly sure it was. But the main thing was the most obvious one."

"What?" everyone chorused.

"There is no way a family wouldn't venture outside early on Christmas morning if it was snowing. There were no footprints, yet everyone sounded wide awake and happy inside. They would have been playing in the snow for sure."

"You're right!" laughed Dad. "We couldn't keep you away from snow when you were young. The odd time it was actually a white Christmas you were outside more than in, even with your new presents."

"Speaking of presents," I began, hating to bring it up but having to solve this most annoying puzzle, "you can own up now about the tree and food. You ate Santa and Rudolph's snacks."

"Max, we swear that we didn't." Mum held Dad's hand, their love as apparent as ever, as she added, "I swear on my life and your father's. We snuck in and put the presents out, but we did not do the tree or eat the food. The tree was already there and we assumed Anxious ate the food."

"Then it's true," giggled Min. "Santa actually came. He really did."

We turned to her and I'm sure we had the same dubious expression, but she flung her arms up, eyes bright, and insisted, "He came because we've been good. Merry Christmas, everyone."

"Merry Christmas!" we chorused.

Chapter 22

By the next day, it felt like a dream. We'd stepped out in the morning to find the snow melting, the sun shining, and David and Gina were already gone. Kev followed soon after.

Mum and Dad didn't get it together until the afternoon, taking an age to sort things out as usual, but it was nice to spend time with them without any drama of the murderous kind.

We heard from Clarence, which was kind of him to think of us, to let us know that Sam had been picked up later that night from the village and hadn't caused a fuss. He felt sorry for him just like we all had, but now it was out of his hands and he was in the system.

Maddie and Roy were straight back to work, keen to get moving with things after the previous day's events. They apologised profusely for seeming off, but put it down to stress and confusion over what jobs took priority at the campsite, which was now their livelihood but very new to them.

After an afternoon stroll with Anxious, Min and I retreated to Vee and sat outside under the new gazebo, chatting about it excitedly and generally fawning over our gifts and how it would be a real game-changer.

"What are you going to do next?" asked Min as we sipped steaming coffees.

"You know what? Even though Mitchell's murder was awful, I think I'm going to stay here for a few months. Really settle in, take it easy, and have a break from travelling."

"By take it easy, do you mean work full-time for Maddie and Roy and help renovate the house and campsite?"

My eyebrows shot up. "How did you know?"

"You aren't the only great amateur detective," she sniggered.

"Or you spoke to Maddie earlier and she told you," I teased.

"Spoilsport! Max, that's a great idea. No more murders and no stress. Wait for spring, enjoy doing something different, and feel more like you have a home."

"I always feel at home in Vee, but a few months staying put should mean no deaths, and that will be great. What I really want to do is something physical though. It'll be good for me, but also Maddie and Roy need the help. I want this to work out for them, so I'm going to help. Will you come and visit now and then?"

"Of course I will! You try to keep me away. I miss you guys already and I haven't even left yet."

"We miss you too. Come any time, and stay as long as you want, and before long it'll be spring, then summer, and we'll see what the warm weather brings." I left it at that, not wanting to push things, or even discuss us getting back together properly by then.

"Thank you for everything, Max. Now, I better get going."

I nodded, as I knew she had work, and this time of year was a busy one for a personal dietitian. We spent an hour just sorting things out, then I drove Min to the train station and we waited until her train left so we could wave her off.

The afternoon saw me sitting outside in the freezing cold, wrapped up with all the layers, but with my Crocs on.

I smiled as I stared down at them and imagined the warmer weather that would be here soon enough. For a few months, I'd work hard, keep warm, and help people out.

Then I'd do a lovely tour wherever the fancy took me, and before long it would be summer.

"Merry Christmas, Anxious."

My best buddy lifted his head, the bell tinkling, the pom-pom bouncing. He'd refused to take it off, and that was fine. Barking to ensure he had my undivided attention, he glanced at my pocket.

With a laugh of pure joy and contentment with my life, I gave him a biscuit, wiggled my toes, and stared out at the field as several campervans pulled up and people began setting up camp.

You couldn't beat the sound of sliding doors or zips opening and closing as it meant freedom. I never tired of the smiles fellow travellers always gave one another, or the comical entertainment as newbies tried to figure out how to erect drive-away awnings, or how on earth you were meant to cook inside your campervan without getting bacon fat splattered all over your newly upholstered interior.

Life didn't get better than this.

Merry Christmas.

And now we get to cook something special. Max did incredibly well sorting out Christmas Dinner for everyone, especially given the circumstances. It might not have been with all the trimmings, but if you want less stress on Christmas Day and especially if you are away in your van, then why not give this a try?

Read on for an incredible one-pot recipe, and a little more about what's next for Max and the gang.

Recipe

Christmas Beef Pot Roast Dinner

Remember, a pot roast isn't just for Christmas…

Ingredients

- Rapeseed oil - 3 tablespoons
- Rolled beef brisket - 1.5kg
- Onion - 2 sliced
- Garlic - 5 cloves, peeled
- Carrots - 4 peeled and halved
- Celery - 2 sticks halved
- Beef stock cube - 1
- Thyme - 1 tsp
- Dijon mustard - 1 tbsp
- Bay leaves - 4
- Red wine - half a bottle of something good enough to drink (after all, there will be half a bottle going spare)
- Potatoes - 1.5kg large floury ones peeled and quartered or small waxy new potatoes left whole and unpeeled
- Baby or chantenay carrots - 500g scrubbed but left whole
- Butter - a good knob
- Salt and freshly ground black pepper to taste

Method

You could use another cut of beef but you want some fatty marbling to get the very best flavour. Make sure the beef has come up to room temperature before you start, and season it well before doing anything else.

I've used red wine as its Christmas, but white wine, beer, or good old stock will be perfectly delicious too.

- Heat 2 tbsp of oil in a very big, heavy pot and brown the beef on all sides. You want a high heat to sear it pretty quickly.
- Once that's done, remove the beef to a plate and reduce the heat to medium. Time to sauté the onion until just starting to turn golden around the edges.
- Add the garlic, halved carrots, and celery and stir until its all shiny and starting to colour.
- Crumble in the stock cube, add the thyme, mustard, bay leaves, and red wine. Stir it all together and then make some room in the pan to nestle your beef back in.
- Top up with 250ml water and bring to a slow simmer. Cover and leave to blip away gently for around three hours. Have a peek (and a stir) every now and again to catch anything that's starting to stick. Around halfway through I like to turn the beef over but I'm not sure its really needed.
- The vegetables by now should be pretty mushy. For a bit more texture we'll add the baby carrots and potatoes for the last hour. Once the time is up, the beef should be shreddably tender and veg should be soft.
- Take the beef out to rest (covered in a foil tent or tea towel) while you sort out the gravy and "roast" potatoes. This will be easiest if you cheat a little and get a big frying pan involved (but by all means decant the gravy and wipe your big pot out and use

that). Discard the bay leaves. You'll need to fish out the potatoes and baby carrots and gently shake them about in a sieve a bit to get them to steam dry a little.

- Heat the remaining oil and butter on a medium-high heat in the frying pan until starting to foam. Then add potatoes and carrots. You'll need to resist the urge to do too much stirring until they are starting to get a golden crust. Shake them around a little until done to your liking.

- Use a potato masher, stick blender, or food processor to incorporate the soft onions, garlic, celery, and softest carrots into the cooking liquid. This is your gravy. Pop it back in the pot and season to taste. You might want to reduce it down a little further, or add some more stock depending on your gravy tastes.

- Serve up your spuds, veg, and shredded beef and top with the delicious gravy.

- *Merry Christmas!*

You really should have something green with this, but of course that's another pan so I'll leave it up to you. Of course bunging some frozen peas in at the end is always a potless option.

You could add some parsnips or swede along with the potatoes. Or make things easier (and pottier) by forgetting the roasties and serving with a huge mound of buttery mash (apparently some folks only have mashed potatoes, and no roasties at all for Christmas, but I'm not sure I believe it).

Don't forget some horse-radish sauce and your paper hats.

From the Author

I hope you found Christmas Corpse fun and entertaining. I certainly had a blast writing it. It was nice to see the other side of vanlife, and I think everyone coped incredibly well. Of course, for some, vanlife is part-time and just the occasional trip, so not as much planning is involved. But for full-time vanlifers there is so much to consider, not least of which is heating and ventilation.

Let's hope Max makes it through the winter and enjoys his time working at the campsite. I'm sure we'll catch up with him right when there's another murder mystery to solve.

Speaking of which…

Are you ready for book 12?

Me too! Order Dead in the Deli now and see what's in store for Max, Anxious, and whoever else turns up.

And what's going on with the graffiti? That's weird, right?

Be sure to stay updated about new releases and fan sales. You'll hear about them first. No spam, just book updates at www.authortylerrhodes.com.

You can also follow me on Amazon www.amazon.com/stores/author/B0BN6T2VQ5.

Connect with me on Facebook www.facebook.com/authortylerrhodes/

Printed in Great Britain
by Amazon

56479553R00118